Soraya

Leon Michaels

Books by Leon Michaels
Stand Alone Action/Adventure

The Path Home

From the Mists of Darkness

Task Force Nemesis

Tales From The Bench

The Echelon Factor

Today is Yesterday's Tomorrow

Stand Alone ScFi

The Morbius Expedition

Random Acts Of Science Fiction

A Rigged Deck

Willem

A Lancer's Tale

Soraya

Post- Apocalyptic

Three Against The Darkness

"The Crane Equation Trilogy"

The Crane Equation: The Early Years

The Crane Equation: Rebuilding a Nation

The Crane Equation: The Crane Legacy

Action/Adventure

"The Black Ops Series"

Operation Damocles

Operation Dokkaebi

Operation Yofune-Nushi

Operation Kartikeya

The Black Orchid

The Twenty-First Special Operations Group: Book One: Family

The Twenty-First Special Operations Group: Book Two: Operators

Operation Heracles

Operation Pandora

Operation Pegasus

ScFi-Action/Adventure

"The Denoyelles Family Saga"

The Hanover Throne

The Bellus Project

The Bellus Legacy

The Bellus Myth

The Bellus Solution

The Bellus Prophecy

The Phoenix Project

The Bellus Curse

Acknowledgements

As Always to my Bride of 47 years who proofreads, edits, comments, and tries not to vomit when she reads my work.

She doesn't deserve the likes of me, but she refuses to shoot me.

This is a work of Fiction. Any similarities to individuals past or present is unintentional and purely a coincidence. Any similarities to any individual in the future is pure Karma.

This page left blank.

Rebellion

Roman stood leaning against a long lance as he watch the remains of the King's army flee before him through the tall grass. Behind him he could hear the cries of the wounded and dying. He was tired and covered in blood, wishing he could lie down and rest.

The battle started when the sun was barely a hands width above the horizon and it was now slowly creeping up to its highest point in the sky. Roman was uneducated, and could not count but was told he had seven hundred and forty-four men at his side when the battle started, and the King's army was figured to be over twice that size.

He turned back to look at the battle field stretching for nearly two leagues behind him at the bodies of friends and foe laid out as the women of his rebellion moved from body to body, checking for those that might be saved, and gathering anything they might use later.

Gundar, one of his captain's walked up beside him, his head wrapped in a blood soaked rag and spoke to Roman.

"Roman, we number two hundred and thirteen now. But for every man that died out here today, they died free men and they killed three times that number of the King's army."

Roman looked at Gundar with tired eyes then back at the fleeing army nearly out of sight.

"Gundar, we were lucky this day. The King's men had no stomach for a fight and did not believe men as poorly armed as we were would stand against them. Let us rest for a time, then we need to see to the burial of our friends and arm ourselves with the spoils of this fight."

Roman walked back into the battlefield to the shallow river which dissected it and just sat down in its flowing waters and allowed the water to wash away most of the blood which covered his body. At one time, the river flowed red with the blood of friends

7

and foe during the battle as the Rebels pushed the King's army back. The water stung his own wounds from numerous cuts, and he was thankful for the fact none of his wounds were deep enough to inhibit his ability to fight or cripple him.

As he sat, splashing water onto his face, his mind slipped back to before he was the unwilling leader of the slave revolt.

Roman was born into slavery, to work in the King's stone quarry. His mother was a slave and it was unknown who his father was. The women who worked in the quarry tended to the needs of the men during the day by keeping them supplied with food and water and tending to their injuries. At night, they tended to the men's other needs without regard. A woman may service as many men as she was able to during the night, which meant if she became with child, it could belong to any of the hundreds of men who slaved in the quarry.

The only education Roman ever received was limited to the tasks he was trained for and the scars across his back attested to the pain he endured before he mastered his trade. Roman was a stone cutter who could shape and smooth large blocks of the white stone they took from the quarry.

His ability to count only extended to the number of fingers on both hands, and all he had to do when shaping a block was follow the red chalk marks placed on the stone by the Quarry Master, removing any need for him to be further educated.

A male child born to a quarry female began carrying tools and other needs by the time they were five annuals old. As they grew, they were assigned a teacher who taught them the specific craft they had to master. If a male child proved too weak, he just disappeared during the night. It was never known if he was moved to a farm, or just killed so as to not be a burden on the food supplies of the quarry.

Females born to the quarry were protected by the threat of strangulation by hanging if they were touched by a male, removing their virginity. When a female grew to the age of bleeding, she was isolated from the others, guarded by the overseers until a fine dressed female came from the palace to view them. The females she selected were taken away, and then those that remained were deflowered by the overseers, and used by them until turned back to the quarry for the slaves to use.

From time to time, after returning to the quarry, a young female might climb to the highest point in the quarry, and throw herself from the peak to her own death below on the jagged rocks. No one tried to stop them from jumping and often just ignored her as it happened. Death was a relief from harsh treatment of the overseers and the hard work within the quarry. Even when females were turned back to the quarry with a swollen belly from carrying a child at a young age, an overseer might use one of them as the male slaves worked around them, throwing her on the ground, or making them take him in her mouth.

There was no calendar for the slaves to say what day it was, and only the change of the seasons to tell him how old they may be. Roman only knew how many annuals he had been alive by his mother when he was ten annuals, almost an annual before her own death from an accident in the quarry while carrying another child in her womb. He did not morn his mother's death but silently rejoiced she was finally free from the hardships she endured there.

Roman figured he was fourteen annuals when he took his first woman on his pallet in the slave hut. She was much older than him, and had recently birthed a female child. He next took one of the rejected young girls, days after being returned to the slave huts. As he grew older, he found the females might come to him, instead of him selecting one to use. It never dawned on him that this might be wrong as it was what he was raised too in the quarry. He was certain he had sired several children over the years as some had his build and looks, but no one ever commented he might be a father of the children that worked around the quarry. When you are born into a life of hardship, you just ignored as much as possible and did what others did to survive.

When Roman was twenty-four annuals, he was taken to the Palace to trim a large stone that had been incorrectly measured by the Quarry Master. The faint markings of the original outline were still present, and they were off about two of Roman's fingers too thick. New markings were in place and he went to work on the large stone block as soon as his tools were unloaded by a Palace slave.

That night, Roman was shown a place to bath and was tended to by a female slave which he took to his bed once he was clean. She serviced him nightly for the several days then a new female was given to him. And unlike the slave huts, where all could see who was being service, he had a room with a door and an actual bed with a straw mattress to sleep on.

But it was here that Roman also saw how the other people of the kingdom lived. People freely walking around in fine clothing, often with slaves following behind them, to tend to their needs. He never saw a single female taken in the open as he did in the quarry, but he did see one pulled into a dark corner and used by her master.

It was here the first seeds of revolt were planted into Roman's mind. He was returning to his quarters one night when he saw one of the slaves kneeling in front of a guard servicing him with their mouth. Unlike previous night's where he had seen this happening, this time something didn't look right and as he looked back over his shoulder he realized the slave was male, not female. He had never seen this in the quarry, and had never been placed into that position when he was young by slave or overseer.

After that night, Roman began to watch things going on around him when he had the moment to look away from what he was doing. He began to see things he had never noticed before as he worked to chisel away the excess material from the block, smoothing it so it would fit in place as tightly as possible in the wall it was to go into when finished.

He was over half way through the cutting and had gone through a handful of females when he was taken to bath and found an older woman, dressed much nicer than the average female slave and another young female standing nude beside her. His female escort removed her plain coverlet and was joined by the second young female in the large tube to bath him. The older female added scents to the water and told him he was not to enjoy either of the females bathing him as he was to service another this night.

Roman became erect as the young females washed him paying attention to his manhood and when he rose out of the water, the older woman smiled and walked over to him and took him in her hand.

"I think in a couple of nights, I shall let you join with me, but not tonight."

She released him then walked over to where water was moving from a spicket in the water. She filled a container then walked back to Roman and poured the water over his erection. He shivered from the effect of the cold, almost chilled water on him and after two more containers, his erection was gone.

He was given a simple wrap to cover himself with and a cloth vest before he was lead from the bath by the elder woman into part of the palace through hidden doors until he found himself in a lust apartment with a large bed with curtains around it. Standing at the foot of the bed was another older woman in a gown so thin he could see her body through it.

Incense burned from holders around the room and Roman was stopped back from the new woman who smiled as she looked at him. His escort removed his vest from behind him then reached around, unfastened his wrap, exposing him to the new woman.

The woman hiked one leg up on the end of the bed as she took hold of a pillar holding up the bed curtain and snapped her fingers. A young girl attended the woman.

"Prepare me for this man."

The girl dropped to her knees and moved close, taking her Mistresses womanhood with her lips. Roman had never seen anything like this and as the girl moved her head, working the woman into desire, Roman became excited and slowly became erect as the woman watched him until she was groaning and closed her eyes, enjoying the treatment of the girl on her. She opened her eyes to see Roman stroking himself and spoke to him.

"Come to me, let me do that for you."

Roman moved to her and she took him in hand as the girl continued her task of preparing the woman for him in bed. Soon the woman was shaking and groaning as she pulled on Roman until he reached up and grabbed one of her breasts, squeezing it hard. The woman cried out and nearly fell over as she experienced her high pleasure.

When she was able to speak, she looked at Roman and told him to use her as he desired. Roman picked her up away from the girl and threw her on the bed, then followed her on it. He took her twice that night with the girls and the other woman watching from outside the curtains. When he finished with her the second time, one girl moved to clean the woman with her mouth as another cleaned Roman before he was told to dress, so he could be taken to his own bed.

The next night, he took the other woman in his own room and the first time he took her, as he had her pinned to his bed with his manhood deep inside the woman, he asked who it was that he serviced the night before. It was then that he discovered he had serviced the Queen.

Roman serviced the Queen twice more before he was finished with his work on the block and serviced the other woman whom he never learned her name, three times.

He watched as the large block of stone was lifted into position and wedged into place, making a near seamless fit. Roman spent one last night in his room with two girls before he was taken back to the quarry the next morning.

When he returned to the quarry he saw it differently than before. His eyes were opened to the fact he was born a slave and never given a chance to be more than that. Why his mother and her mother and the possible father's were slaves had no meaning to him other than once placed in that position, they had no other choice in life. Even the open using of the females by the males suddenly became vulgar to him even after enjoying the slave girls in the Palace. They had no choice to whom they gave themselves too, and he had little choice in who he was to service.

Quietly he spoke of his time at the Palace, the things he saw and did there. His own use of females became noticed as he before he would take one to his pallet when he desired, but now, they came to him and he often just held them as they slept so another would not use the female.

Roman looked at the overseers with an eye to determine if they had the strength to stand against the quarry workers, even with the swords and lances they had available. No, the strength of the men developed through long days of working in the stone had hardened the slaves, made them much stronger than the overseers.

He quietly talked to the smiths, the men who formed the tools from steel used by cutters like himself to see if they could make swords and other weapons. If the slaves fought for their freedom, they would need more weapons than they could take from the overseers.

It was nearly two months by the planet calendar that Roman and twenty men broke out of the back of the slave hut, and through the crude stockade, to silently move on the overseers that were standing the night watch. Once they were dealt with, they moved on the overseers quarters armed with the weapons and anything they could use as a weapon.

Although outnumbered, and not trained to use the swords they had obtain, they were able to overcome the overseers as some were killed while still asleep in their beds, some with female slaves next to them. By daylight, the quarry was in the hands of the slaves and the smiths were making their forges hot to turn tools into swords and knives.

Days later when a train of wagons arrived to take the cut stone blocks back to the Palace, Roman's men took the train, freeing the slaves that were with it. In doing so, they learned of other locations were the slaves worked to provide for those living in the Palace city.

They had freed three farms before word finally made it to the Palace. The Rebels as they were called were moving to another farm when they were confronted by the King's army. The Rebels had few weapons to match the army, but they improvised with sharpened long shafts, axes, shovels, anything they could fight with.

This was the battle that Roman was cleaning from his body. As the King's men fell, their weapons were picked up by men who had makeshift weapons and entered into the fray. After years under the whip, these men fought hard and death for them was only a relief from their pain.

Roman left the water and just stood by the stream to watch his men also clean themselves. He had to laugh knowing that the river went to the Palace city and he wondered if it would still run red with the blood of the fallen and that which was cleaned from his men's bodies.

One of the women approached him with a burden in her arms.

"Roman, these belonged to their leader who fell in battle. I cleaned the blood from them, so you could have them."

She laid the bundle down then kneeled with it and began handing him things. The first was a helm which had a slight dent in it. Roman tried it on the find it was too small for him. He tossed it down as she handed him a breast plate. It was scarred but whole. He looked at the woman who grinned.

"Their leader's head was not attached to his body."

Again, the breast plate was too small.

"Woman, what is your name as I do not recognize you?"

14

"I am called Domma, and I come from the farms."

"Thank you Domma, but I think all of these things are too small. Find someone they will fit."

"Yes, Roman, I will. Now here, these should fit you."

She handed up a sword in a scabbard and belt with a pouch and knife attached. He wrapped the wide belt around his waist and fastened it then adjust the placement of the sword and knife. He pulled the sword to find it of high quality with a few nicks in the blade, but serviceable.

"It is a fine blade Domma, yet it did its owner no good in the end."

"Maybe it was in the hands of the wrong man this day?"

"Domma, go tell the women that once they are sure there are none of our people in need of care to gather all weapons and stack them here where I stand. We will need wagons from the farm behind us to transport our wounded and those weapons back to the farm as we rest and make plans. Also bring shovels so we can bury our dead. Go now and do this for me."

"I shall Roman." She turned away then back. "Roman, I am yours tonight if you desire."

"Go Domma, we can consider that once we see to those that need our help."

It would take three days to bury the dead even with help from the men from the farm who had not fought in the battle. Domma saw to Roman's needs during this time and during the move to the next farm where they found the overseers had fled, leaving the slaves behind except for a few young girls they took for their use.

They found another farm completely abandoned as the overseers had herded the slaves to the Palace city to prevent them from joining the revolt.

Ten days after the battle, his forward men, his scouts reported Calvary moving towards them. Roman caught the Calvary in a wooded area, ambushing them, and when the battle was over, he now had horses and even more weapons to supply the men from the farms. It was figured less than twenty of the Calvary survived to ride back to the Palace.

Two days later, Roman sat astride a horse on a ridge looking towards the Palace in the distance. He spoke to Gundar at his side without looking at him.

"Gundar, we have been lucky as the King's army has no heart for battle, but I've been to that city and it's walls will not be easy to overcome."

"What are you thinking Roman?"

Roman looked down at the grain growing beneath the horses and had an idea.

"Gundar, we set fire to these fields, let the smoke blow to the city as we move around it and free the farms near the Palace, and burn the crops while gathering all we can to feed ourselves. We starve those that would enslave us. Go spread the word and see that it is done."

Spies

After Gundar left to carry out his orders, Roman just sat on his horse, looking at the Palace thinking he had taken on more than he was capable of dealing with. His meager army of slaves had been lucky up to now as the King's army was not prepared to fight me who did not care if they lived or died.

Something caught his eye to his right, something that seemed to shimmer, but when he turned to look in that direction it disappeared. He looked for a moment, then gave a heavy sigh, reined his horse around and headed back to their camp in the woods to get something to eat, and prepare for the next step in freeing the slaves on the other farms surrounding the Palace.

Senior Lieutenant Soraya Khan of the Hayutan Navy stood, watching the one called Roman ride back towards their camp. She looked around at the pickets who were watching the Palace to see if anyone would come out and challenge the Rebels, then slowly moved back into the trees, then towards her one person survey craft. Soraya was part of a five person survey team which had discovered this world over a year before during the expansion of the Federation into the unknown universe.

As she moved to her survey vessel, she was concerned the cloaking suit she was wearing had failed, but if it had, he would have said or done something. The suit was fairly new technology compared to the old cloaking devices the Hayutans first used.

Soraya admired the small ship she used to come to the surface as it was a modified Viper fighter, except it only carried two Askook V missiles on its wingtips, and no nose cannon. Besides being almost two-thirds the size of the original Viper, it landed with skids instead of wheels, leaving less visible foot print in the soil. Plus, it did not need a ladder to enter the cockpit.

In keeping with the use of reptiles when naming these single seated crafts, her ship was of the Krait class, another poisonous viper from Earth. It took her almost an hour to get to her ship as she avoided several people in the woods gathering up firewood and berries. She looked around the vessel to make sure no one had stumbled onto it, even though it was cloaked. Once strapped into her cockpit, she had the AI run a sensor check to insure no humans were within one hundred meters of her when she lifted.

The vessel she was to link up with in orbit was a special built Monarch Class Survey Ship based upon the old Scout ships. It was half again longer and had a separate bay in the rear especially for the Krait aircraft to utilize as a hanger.

Soraya was part of a five person crew whose only purpose was to locate Class M Planets, survey them and report back to Hayutan Fleet Headquarters on the status of the planet. Since this planet was inhabited, they had to do a comprehensive survey, to include collecting DNA when and where possible of the inhabitants, then make an estimate of how to make contact with the people of the planet.

There were several problems with this planet in that it was the first discovered with inhabitants since Duke Carlos discovered Marta's World and Panterra outside the Southern Rim. This planet was a year, at high boost, distance from Panterra.

Then there was the fact that the inhabitants were living in what on Earth was called the Iron Age. Early in mankind's venture into space, a similar civilization was discovered on the planet Zyra, or what was once known as Hawking's World. The sudden intrusion of modern man into that civilization nearly wiped them out until steps were taken to restrict contact and slowly bring them into a modern world.

There were laws written and abided by concerning contact with discovered civilizations. And both the Fleet and Federation were strict in enforcing those laws.

Soraya guided her Krait into the landing position to her survey ship, the Searcher, then turned controls over to the AI to execute the actual landing inside the small hanger bay. Once inside the bay, the hanger was closed and sealed, an atmosphere introduced into it and Soraya climbed out of the vessel. She visually checked the deck locks on her skids before entering the main part of the ship.

Because of the size of the vessel, and the regulation that two crewmembers must always be awake and on the Command Deck, there were only three bunks aboard the Searcher. Today only one of them had its privacy screen up and that could mean any number of bodies were in the bunk at the moment. The privacy screens blocked out sight and sound giving a couple complete privacy for sexual activity, or just one person undisturbed sleep. Only an Action or Battle Stations alarm could be heard inside the screen.

The five person crew of the Searcher consisted of two men and three women. Lieutenant Commander Henry "Hank" Dodge was in command. Senior Lieutenant Martha "Marty" Miller was Exec. Sub-Lieutenant Donald "Donnie or Don" Plowright was the Sensor Tech, with Sub-Lieutenant Constance "Connie" Bergdahl as Communications.

Soraya was the Survey Specialist of the crew. She actually started her military career in the Hayutan Marines as an Intelligence Specialist before being sent to the Fleet Academy and obtaining her Advance Degree in Xeno-Biology. Many mistook her Intelligence Specialty as someone who set behind a desk and drew conclusions from field reports. Soraya was one of those trained to be out ahead of field troops, gathering intelligence to make their movements simpler and smoother. She had attained the rank of Sergeant as a Marine during three separate operations against Raiders and Slavers up in the Northern portion of the South Rim.

There was no one in the common area when she passed through it to the Bridge and she found Hank and Connie at their stations, telling Soraya that Martha and Don were sharing a bunk during their off time. Hank spoke before she could.

"Soraya, we have orders to link up with the Heavy Cruiser Bridgeport, and do a complete briefing on the situation down below. I know you are probably tired, but you need to get your notes together for this, since this is what you do."

"No Problem Hank, it'll only take a few minutes to write todays observations down. Do I have time for a couple hours before we meet with the Bridgeport?"

"Sure, as long as you are ready for the briefing, take what you can get. We'll wake you before we dock."

"Thanks Hank."

She went back into the common area and sat down at one of the computers available there and quickly wrote out her report, double checked it, saved it to the mission log, then transmitted it back to Fleet Headquarters on Hayuta.

Once that was taken care of, she stripped to her panties and crawled onto the first bunk, activated the Privacy Curtain, and almost immediately went to sleep.

Hank took a deep sigh as he watched her strip and get into the bunk thinking she was much better looking than the other two females, yet she was celibate. He just put her out of his mind and plotted a course to rendezvous with the Bridgeport.

As Soraya rested, Roman was sitting with an old man named Eli from one of the farms that kept the farms records. He was teaching Roman mathematics and how to read and write. The old man also became his chronicler. When Roman made a decision or rule, Eli wrote it down so later if anyone wished to understand what was said, he had it exactly in Roman's words.

Six hours after Soraya laid down, she walked into the Bridgeport's conference room to find the Sector Commander, Commodore Faria present. Soraya found herself the center of attention since she was the Survey Officer for this planet.

Commodore Faria opened the meeting once introductions were out of the way.

"Lieutenant Khan, have you discovered a name for this planet besides our catalog number of QB-5547?"

"No Sir, I have not."

He moved some papers around in front of him as if checking his notes.

"Very well. Now according to your reports, these people speak a version of Spanglish, is that correct?"

"Yes Sir."

"Alright, let's cut to the chase here. Lieutenant, in your reports you advise the Federation that these people have a level of open debauchery unknown for eons to mankind. Care to explain that better."

Soraya put a micro-disk into the hologram control in front of where she was sitting and selected a group of stills from the videos she had been taking with each investigation on the surface. She showed them in slow sequence so there was no mistaking what was happening at the moment the video was taken.

There were stills taken inside the actual throne room where the King was raping young girls and a couple of young boys on or behind the throne on a small couch. Guards and other retainers could be seen in the backgrounds of the stills. She paused for a moment on one particular still.

"Commodore, what you have seen is the King raping slaves as young as twelve for his own pleasure, but this girl was given to the King by a merchant, so he could receive a grant. The girl is the merchants daughter."

"Turn it off please." The Commodore asked.

"Commodore, I have hours of video of guards raping young girls in the halls of the Palace. Guards raping girls in the farm fields or in the stone quarry. Female slaves seem to have only a single purpose, and that is to be used to produce more slaves from their wombs."

She paused for a moment.

"Once a girl has been deflowered, violated, then they are used even by the male slaves for pleasure. I watched one of the King's minor female retainers go to a farm and from observation, young girls, just reaching puberty, were selected and taken back to the Palace. Those not selected were raped by the guards that night, and kept by the guards until they tired of them, then put them back into the slave population. I have video of young girls committing suicide once back in the population due to their treatment."

"Lieutenant Khan, you are commended for maintaining self-control under the conditions you have described. I know what the regulations you are working under state, but I do not think I could have remained neutral based on what you have said here today."

"Thank you, Sir, it has only been my oath to the Fleet that has stayed my hand."

He moved a paper, then picked one up as to read it before further speaking.

"Tell me about this Roman individual."

Soraya told the Commodore everything she knew and had observed concerning Roman. She explained that how he was able to get the quarry slaves to revolt was unknown since she had mostly been focused on the Palace city and the surrounding farms. She had seen him in the quarry the few times she had visited there, but never gave him much thought other than he was bigger than the average worker.

The night that the slaves revolted in the quarry, they just happened to be scanning the surface and saw unusual activity in the quarry and she went down to examine the situation. The revolt was already over by the time she had arrived with all of the guards dead at the hands of the slaves. It was well after daylight that she was able to determine that this Roman individual was giving the orders.

She spent over an hour giving a brief event by event account up to date with video in places to emphasize the strength of the revolt. The three minutes of the first battle with the King's army showed how the slaves were fearless in their attack and pursuit of the fleeing army. One clip showed Roman moving through the ranks of the King's soldiers with two swords, slashing and cutting men down as he moved forward.

Once the briefing was complete, she just sat quietly, waiting for any further questions. It was a long time before the Commodore spoke.

"Everyone clear the room except for Lieutenant Khan."

Once everyone had left and the door closed, the Commodore sat up straight in his chair and looked at her.

"Lieutenant Khan how are you mentally. What you have witnessed has to have been taking a toll on you."

"I'm alright Commodore. It was hard at first, but with the revolt, except for the bloodshed, it has given me hope for these people. I was able to get close enough to hear Roman forbid the taking of any female without their permission, where in the past, a man would just take one by the arm to his bedding and use her even if she was in her cycle or pregnant."

"Lieutenant, you know I am part Centaurian, but such blood letting during those battles is unknown to even the Centaurians. What do we do now with these people?"

"Sir, that is not for me to say."

"Lieutenant Khan, there is a plan that depends on you. But before I introduce it to you, I want you to spend some time with the Psych Doctors to insure your stability for your part in this plan. As I have said, what you have seen has to have played heavily on you and I need to know if you are up to the next part of your mission here. I cannot in good conscious send you into that mission without knowing you can deal with it. I hope I have made my position clear on this."

"Commodore, I have given some thought to my own sanity at times, so I find no offense in your orders Sir."

"Speak of this to no one because the one part of the plan I can tell you now is that we or I have been ordered to violate Fleet and Federation Regulations in this matter. Go now and see the Docs, and tell those waiting in the corridor to come back in, please."

Soraya pulled the micro-disk from the control, stood, nodded to the Commodore, then did as he instructed.

As Soraya was involved with the Psych Docs, Roman was executing his own plans as he moved on the farms surrounding the Palace. His movements were quick now that his men were becoming mounted from horses taken from the farms, moving as cavalry instead of infantry, quickly moving from farm to farm, often hitting a farm, and taking his men to the next as one small group stayed behind to free and organize the slaves.

He caught one group of overseers trying to flee with loads of grain and young girls, some who had not yet been deflowered, and put them all to the sword. At another farm, the overseers were trying to kill the slaves before they also ran, with the slaves fighting back with their bare hands.

During the three solar days that Soraya was involved with the Psych Docs, Roman had nearly encircled the Palace city.

For Soraya, the time was a haze as the Docs put her in a semi-coma to carefully peel back her mind to discover the person inside the body. They were not allowed to inhibit or change her mental state, only look into it and determine her status, unlike dealing with enemies of the Federation or criminals.

By the fourth day, they knew Soraya almost better than she knew herself, and once it was determined she was stable, dedicated to her profession, they then enhanced her knowledge with the things she would need for the mission the Commodore was going to present to her. She still had her free will and the ability to turn down the mission, but it was easier once in her condition to implant the information then going back a second time.

As Soraya set quietly in the conference room alone with the Commodore as he laid out the next part of the mission to this world, Roman closed off any avenue of escape from the Palace city. Fields were burning, destroying crops needed by the city people as smiths forged more weapons for the freed slave army.

Soraya accepted her assignment, and the risks involved with an advancement to Lieutenant Commander. Her mission was to infiltrate the Slave Army, get close to Roman, and hopefully advise him on conduct and tactics where possible in ending the King's rule and stabilizing the world in chaos.

The first thing she had to do was to free a farm further south of the Palace that Roman had not ventured towards. In doing so, she would bring those freed slaves into Roman's army as she establish herself.

In preparation for this mission, as she was involved with the Docs, craftsmen aboard the Bridgeport has fashioned her clothing, leather trousers and vests for her to wear. She had a helm that contained communications and an AI which would assist her especially in keeping in contact with the Searcher.

Her edged weapons were fashioned as the ones on the planet, except made from stronger metals. And she would carry a concealed five millimeter pistol with silencer. But the one weapon she would carry was one that could change the tide of war, a weapon she had not seen yet, and that was a long bow.

The Searcher landed a kilometer from the farm so selected as her start point, and she left it with a crude, cloth pack with other items she might need as she walked to the farm to begin her mission. It was just after midnight as she started her journey, and by daylight, the overseers of the farm were dead from a single bullet to the head as they slept or stood watch.

Soraya moved so quietly that the females lying next to the men she killed, never stirred as she eliminated them as they slept.

Integration

Soraya stood on a wagon seat as she addressed the gathering of freed slaves and told them about the revolt and the army surrounding the Palace city. When asked where she came from, she pointed to the mountains behind them and said that was where she was born and raised as a free soul. Then when one of the men asked her how and what they would fight with, she just smiled.

She had not killed the farm manager or his wife, but had injected them with a sleep drug then tied them up before waking the slaves. The manager was nude and tied to a post about sixty paces from where she was standing and in view of the gathering. When Soraya had called the people together, she told them to arrange themselves, so everyone could see her, the tall men and women to the back, and the shorter ones up front. Being of the slave mentality still, it was an easy task to accomplish.

Soraya pulled a long shaft from her quiver hanging off her waist, turned to the manager and fixed the shaft to her long bow. Her pull was slow, so the people could see what she was doing and when she was content with her aim, she released the arrow to find its mark. It hit the manager just to the left of his sternum, piercing his heart and killing him almost instantly. When his body slumped against the ropes holding him to the post a cheer went up from the crowd.

"I will teach you how to make and use this weapon for hunt with for food and to kill your enemies. I only ask you swear an oath to me, not as your master, but as your leader. And let no man or woman enslave you again."

A cry went up from the crowd. Then a single female voice was heard.

"What of the witch of the manor? What of her?"

Soraya looked at the nude wife of the manager tied to another post.

"Hear my words people and do not forget them. No woman will be taken unless she wants to be used on a man's bedding. This includes the witch as you have named her. Kill her quick, or release her as she stands to nature, but she will not be abused as you once were. Anyone who violates my word will feel the edge of my sword. No female will be used to satisfy the desires of a man unless she also desires such contact."

At first only the women cheered at Soraya's words then the men joined in. One of the women took a long blade from the man standing next to her, walked over to the witch and drove the blade into her heart. Once she was sure the woman was dead, she pulled the blade out and turned to look at Soraya.

"The witch would make us take her with our mouths to please her and she was always dirty, often after she had taken her man inside of her. Never again, My Lady!"

Soraya felt no pity for the manager's wife if what the female had said was true.

"Listen carefully. First, bury the dead as this farm still has use to the fighters at the Palace city. Craftsmen gather your tools and be ready for guidance in making bows and long shaft arrows for them. Smiths, once all are buried, forge blades for all needing them, and points for the arrows. Time is short and there is much to do before our journey to join with those who are fighting and dying for your freedom. Go, see to what I have spoken."

The people bent to the tasks they were given, and Soraya moved amongst them looking for the natural leaders. When she spoke to one man and he kneeled in front of her, she reached down and told him to never kneel to another person again. He was free to stand, and speak to them as equals.

She took her long bow to the wood craftsmen, the men who made or repaired the objects made from wood around the farm, and laid it out so they could copy it. She stood back and watched them test the flew and strength before deciding which wood to use to duplicate the bow. They examined the long shaft arrows and once more decided how to make them. They called for a woman, a weaver and they talked about how to make the bow string. Soraya told them not to worry about making their bows exactly the same for now, she would teach them volley fire which in a battle with massed forces will work as well as her accuracy with her bow.

It took two days for the wood crafters to develop a good, strong bow and the weaver wove four different strings which Soraya tested, breaking two and on the fourth, she proclaimed it would do but if the weaver could make it just a bit tighter, it would be better. Two hours later the weaver produced a string that Soraya felt would stand up to the strain and provide the energy needed to launch a long shaft a hundred meters if need be. Soraya then rubbed the string with cold wax from a candle, rubbing it into the mesh, showing the weaver what needed to be done to the next cords she wove.

The arrows were more difficult, but once the pattern was developed and the craftsmen knew what to do, the making of them came quick. The smiths made the arrow heads, melting light steel and pouring it into molds carved from stone, then working them on a foot powered grinding wheel until complete. They understood each arrowhead needed to be as close to exactly the same in order for all arrows to fly true.

On the fifth day, Soraya gave her first class in using the bow at thirty paces. Grain sacks stuffed with straw provided the targets and after several flights of arrows, her fledging archers understood how to at least hit the sack. Hitting it in the center would take practice.

Quivers were made for the arrows and belts for the knives as they prepared for the journey to meet up with the other freed slaves around the Palace. Sacks of grain were loaded into the wagons as was chickens and hogs in cages built for that purpose. Everything they might need was loaded into the half dozen wagons from blankets to cook pots, to coverage in case it rained.

Soraya was getting updates from the Searcher on what was happening at the Palace City. Low level viewing of the inside of the city walls showed a population on the verge of panic. When the

28

King's army sortied out to confront the Rebels, they were beaten back into the city gate after loosing nearly half the army. But it had cost the Rebels also.

The Rebels piled the enemy dead up near the gates, covered them with crude oil which seeped from the ground nearby and set the pile on fire. Roman had the funeral pyre set where the wind would blow the smell of burning flesh back into the city.

The next morning, two nude bodies were hanging from the city wall. Hanging by their neck. One a young girl, the other a young boy. It was proclaimed over the wall that two would be hung each day the Rebels held siege to the city. Roman only commented to his people that the two that were hung were finally put out of their pain of slavery.

Soraya estimated it would take three days for her group to reach the Palace city. The road was well laid out and worn from transporting food to the city so there was no concern about getting lost. They were loading the last of the supplies when the Searcher advise Soraya of the hangings.

Three days for a slow moving wagon train, or twelve hours at a cautious pace for riders on horseback. She told Trent, the smith, to finish loading and take the group to the city as she was taking six of her best archers and riding ahead to smooth the path for them.

Each archer had a full quiver, over twenty arrows each when they left the farm. They also had bread and smoked meat to eat on the way and heavy bladders of water, one for them, and one for their horse. They also added a half bag of grain for each horse tied to the back of the saddle with their blankets.

It was a slow start as most had never ridden a horse before but by the time they had covered nearly half the distance, the men had settled into an understanding of riding.

Soraya road in the lead listening to reports from the Searcher and often listening to soft music to pass the time. Her archers were behind her riding two abreast talking about how it felt to be free to ride in such a manner.

It was past dark when Soraya was stopped by the first of Roman's picket's, watching them ride from the rear of their area. When she was advised that she was close to the pickets by the Searcher, she told her archers to keep their hands free and to make no moves against the people they would meet on the road.

"Stop, who comes this way!" The picket shouted.

"I am Soraya, a friend and I bring allies in the battle against the King."

"Toss down your weapons and come forward."

"I toss down my weapons for no man. Call forth Roman so we can speak, or I will shave off your manhood while you cry for your mother!"

The picket came forward with a long lance and had it point towards Soraya. When it came close enough, she reached out and grabbed it behind the lance head, jerked it to her, then shoved it back hard against the man's chest, knocking him off his feet.

"Little man, you threaten me again, and I will feed that lance to your ass until it comes out your mouth. Summon Roman!"

What no one could see was a thin visor that had dropped over Soraya's eyes from her helm giving her night vision. She could see three men total including the one slowly getting up off the ground. The two men further back were talking to each other then one turned towards the encampment and called for Roman. In the distance, another cry with up for Roman.

Roman was sitting with Eli learning his mathematics when the cry for him came to his ears. He stepped from his shelter.

"Who calls for Roman?"

"Roman, it is the guards at the South road that calls for you."

Came a voice out of the darkness.

"Send word that I am coming to them."

Soon Soraya heard the call that Roman was on his way. She watched the men in front of her as the one she had knocked down was rubbing his chest where the butt of the lance had struck him.

It was several minutes before she saw Roman and several other men walking down the road from the camp. She swung her leg over the horses head and hopped off the mare, then moved towards the oncoming men. As she came to the picket guards she stopped and looked at the one she struck.

"Little man give caution to your thoughts. Your thoughts of revenge against me will cause you nothing but pain and grief before your death."

Roman was close enough by this time to hear what she had said, and he stopped, unsure who this person was even if her voice sounded like a females.

"I am Roman, who are you?"

"I am Soraya, and I come to offer you help in your quest against the King."

"I can see men on horses but cannot tell how many you have brought."

"I have brought six with me and another one hundred and eleven are behind, bringing wagons of grain and other foods for your army. We rode ahead to clear the way for them."

"Where are they from, these wagons of food?"

"From a farm about forty leagues from here. It will still take another day or more for them to arrive."

"So, you and your six men freed a farm?"

"No Roman, I freed the farm. The six men with me were once slaves to the farm."

"HA!" Came a statement from one of the pickets.

Soraya reached behind her back, and pulled her scimitar from its upside down scabbard. The Fleet engineers had made the scabbard so that the sword locked into position, would not fall out unless jerk in a specific manner which she had practiced for hours before dropping to the planet. It also had engraving in the blade and had stones set into the engravings that glowed a bright green in the dark.

Even the metal of the blade edge was treated to glow in the dark and the thin line of green almost looked like fire as she brought the blade up for all to see. Everyone including Roman stepped back as she turned to the pickets.

"Do you doubt me little man?"

"Men stay your tongues as the Lady Soraya is here to help in your quest. Lady Soraya, please return your blade to safe keeping and we shall talk."

Soraya smiled to herself that she had sold her bonafides to Roman and the others. In a world where men had dominated for centuries, she knew she had to prove herself as quickly as possible. The strike of the lance on the picket, and now the drawn sword with its green fire like appearance would soon travel from tent to tent telling all that a female unlike they had never seen before was in camp to help them.

"Forgive me Lord Roman, but I am weary of travel and short of temper this evening."

"Then come, let us share tea and talk."

Soraya returned the sword to its scabbard, then turned to her archers.

"Dismount and lead your horses. Let us follow Lord Roman to a more peaceful place."

At Roman's shelter, she had her archers hobble their horses, feed and water them then for them to eat before lying down for the night. In the faint candle light of his shelter, Roman was able to get a good look at this female that had not only bested one of his men, but had threatened all three with a magic blade.

But he was not ready for what he saw when she removed her helm and loosened her jerkin. Soraya was wearing a leather halter with her torso bare to the top of her leather pants. The strap holding the sword to her back seemed to cut between her breasts, making them more pronounced then normal. He could not be sure the color of her eyes, but they seemed bright compared to the women he had come to know. And her hair light, was like the stalks of grain in the fall at harvest time.

Roman introduced Eli to Soraya then produced two cups of tea, hot from the small fire inside his shelter.

"Where are you from Lady Soraya?"

"Its just Soraya and I come from the mountains to the South. A man who claimed he was once an overseer on a farm you freed passed into where I was and told of the revolt, so I came to see if I could be of help."

"Where is this man now?"

"Feeding the crows. He thought he could take advantage of me in the dark. He was a long time dying."

"Interesting Soraya. How do you plan of placing your people into the army here?"

"I don't Roman. I bring with me knowledge unknown to you and the King's army. Tomorrow morning, I shall show you some of what I bring, and how I intend to use it to open the gates to the Palace. Until then be content that I am here to help you, not kill you."

33

Roman looked at Soraya then laughed a deep belly laugh. When he eased the laughter, he spoke again.

"Why do I think that your words were in jest, yet you are more than capable in carrying them out?"

"You will learn that also in the morning. Now I think rest is in order as tomorrow is going to be full of surprises."

He looked at her and smiled.

"Soraya, would it be improper of me to ask if you would spend the night with me?"

Soraya stood and touched his face then pulled her hand back.

"Roman you are a handsome man, but I am untouched by man and will stay that way until I find a man who excites me in a way I have never felt before. Sadly, you are not that man. Fair evening Roman, I shall see you long before sunrise as I intend to be at the city gates before the sun is above the horizon."

She left the tent with her helm in hand and walked to where her archers had bedded down. Steffen, her best archer had laid out her bedroll and she removed her sword and belt before laying down. It was a far evening and the air felt nice on the exposed parts of her skin.

No, she thought, Roman did not excite her at all. But the man who would excite her was on this world if the prophets of her childhood was correct. Then she thought about the Psych Docs and their entry into her mind. Did they learn of that part of her, or was she able to conceal it as she had concealed other things over the years? If they had learned of her heritage, she would not be here.

After a few minutes, she put her helm back on and told the AI to waken her in plenty of time to eat and ride to the city gates before sunrise. The AI would also alert her to any human who came near enough to her bedding to be of risk to her. It would ignore her own men as they had seen her kill one man and helped bury others

34

she had killed. In this they feared her as much as they respected her choices not to bed any of the men she had freed.

When she woke, Soraya had to relieve her bladder. She woke Steffen and told him to come with her and why. He was going to guard her while she relieved herself in the woods. He pulled his boots on and grabbed his sword then followed her. He stood with his back to her watching one direction as she could watch the other while relieving herself.

Back at the sleeping pads, the others had awoken from hearing Soraya talking to Steffen and one of the men was breaking out the things to cook a grain paste for breakfast as others gather small pieces of dead wood for the fire.

Soraya moved away from the men and contacted the Searcher to get updated on events during the night. The Searcher was now in a stationary orbit above the city and could see out beyond the Rebel lines. Except for the exchange of pickets and sentries, it had been a quiet night even in the city.

The men were eating as Soraya moved back to the fire and Hammel, the man who cooked the meal handed Soraya a bowl of the grain paste and a mug of tea. She sat down with them and ate as she told them what she had planned for this morning. The one called Derstin, collected the now dirty bowls and wooden spoons and washed them in hot water that had been heating while they ate.

As Soraya was finishing her tea, Roman walked up behind her. No one spoke as they recognized him in the light from the fire, but Soraya spoke before he did as her AI identified him as he approached and whispered that information in her ear.

"Did we wake you Roman?"

"No, how did you know it was me?"

"It is good you are here, we are about to leave once Derstin finishes with his task. If I am right, we shall be at the gates before sun up."

"My horse is ready as is my men."

"Roman, you have no need for your men this morn, except to witness what we bring to you. Steffen see to the men stringing their bows and prepare yourselves."

Soraya stood and turned to Roman, then walked past him to her horse. She pulled her unstrung bow from its thin scabbard and strung it then checked to make sure it was properly notched.

"Soraya, the bowls are clean." Derstin called to her.

"Unhobble the horses and let us go visit the city gates."

As they rode past the rack were lances were standing, each man leaned over and grabbed one. As they rode they tied cloth to the butt of the lance shaft. Roman had to catch up to them and as he passed the men, he wondered why they were doing that, tying cloth to the shafts. Just before they cleared the camp perimeter, Soraya grabbed a torch from a post and continued on her mission to be at the gates before sunup.

"Soraya why did the men tie cloth to the ends of the lance shafts?"

"You'll see Roman, be patient."

"Does it have to do with the bend pieces of wood all of you are carrying?"

"Roman, be quiet, you'll see soon enough."

Even though she chided him, her tone was light, almost cheerful. Roman just looked at her from time to time as they rode, thinking if she was as aggressive on a bed as she was with men who annoyed her, he was not sure if he wanted to bed her as she might injure him in a playful manner.

As they rode in silence, Roman thought he heard Soraya talking but she held the torch between them and it was hard to see if her lips were even moving. Soraya was talking to the Searcher who

36

was not only advising her of any opposition in front of them, but guiding her to the most advantages spot to preform her demonstration.

The city walls were only eight meters high which was still more than enough height to hang a person, but was not so high to prevent a long shaft arrow from going over it which was her plan. There were several small gates around the city, but this gate was the main entrance, the only gate large enough for wagons to enter and exit from. This was the gate that needed to be taken in time.

When the Searcher advised her that she was in the proper location, she spread her archers out in front of the wall just to the right of the gate. Her visor was down so she could see anyone on the wall looking down at them. She went down the line as the men drove the lances into the ground and lit the cloths afire, then rode to her spot.

Tied to the men's saddles was a special quiver and from it they drew specially constructed arrows for this mission. The ends still had arrow heads on them, but pushed down on it and onto the shafts were what on old Earth was called cat o'nine tails, a fuzzy plant that had been soaked in petroleum.

The men just sat, arrows ready to lite and fire over the wall on command. Soraya drew a normal arrow and watched the top of the wall. Soon a soldier moved into her vision and she was quick to draw and release the arrow. The man cried out as he was struck in the chest and since he was leaning out to view the happenings outside the wall, he tumbled over the wall to land at the base of it in clear view of Roman and the others in the faint, morning light.

Soraya drew again, and another man fell, this time backwards as his screams seemed to alert the guard.

"Light your arrows and ready yourself!" She commanded.

Soraya looked down the line of men and saw they had learned their lessons well.

"Release!"

The flight of six flaming arrows flew over the wall with ease and the men took another from the quiver and fired them at their own pace until the eight arrows each man was carrying were over the wall and burning. She had told them not to aim at the same point with each arrow, but to spread them out as best they could.

Cries came over the walls as some arrows made contact with flesh and others hitting the wood shingles of the structures on the other side of the wall. Soon flames could be seen rising above the wall.

"Archers be ready and pick your targets." Soraya commanded.

Roman sat fascinated at what he has witnessed from Soraya and the men she called archers. As the flames grew on the other side of the wall, any man moving on the wall was silhouetted and the archers fired upon them. Often two archers firing on the same target.

This went on for several minutes until Soraya called a stop firing. She looked along the wall and saw a head barely peeking over it. She pointed to that individual.

"You, on the wall. Give this message to your King. If we see another slave hung from the walls, we will return and burn the city to the ground."

"Yes, I hear your words and will give them to King Harold."

"Do that and maybe fortune will smile on you and you will live another day."

Soraya drew another arrow and fired it over the wall. Seconds later a scream came from inside the walls and she smiled as her AI was linked to the Searcher and gave her the proper position to fire from causing her arrow to strike a man who was tossing buckets of water onto the fire in an attempt to put it out. Dead or alive did not matter to Soraya as those who witnessed her arrow striking the man would tell of the magic shafts flying over the wall to kill or injure.

On command, the men pulled up the lances and knocked off the remains of the burning cloths, then formed up to follow Soraya back to the Rebel encampment. Roman just followed behind, looking back at the city from time to time to see that the fire was spreading. About six hundred meters from the walls Soraya stopped and turned back to the city.

"Steffen, you and Hammel return to the gates, stay back further but within bow range. Remind them from time to time of my words, but do not waste many long shafts. Derstin and Anton will relieve you before the mid-day meal."

The two men reined their horses around and returned to the wall as Soraya continued back to the camp. At Roman's shelter, they dismounted, and the men began making a shelter for all of them, including Soraya. Roman finally moved to Soraya.

"Mistress Soraya, what magic is this you have brought with you?"

"It is not magic Roman, it is a simple weapon which I am surprised neither you nor the King's army know of. Be patient, as when my wagons arrive, my craftsmen will teach yours how to make such a weapon and we shall teach your men how to use it. Until then, leave us in peace for a time, then we shall talk again."

"Yes Mistress."

"Roman, I am not a mistress, I am just Soraya. Learn that lesson and we shall be friends."

"Yes Soraya."

As Roman walked away, the Comm Unit built into her helm lightly buzzed, then Hank's voice from the Searcher was heard.

"Soraya, if you keep putting him down, he's going to rebel against you and whatever your plans might be for those people."

She looked around to see if she was isolated enough to speak.

"Commander, he has been a slave all his life, he needs to know how to deal with someone outside that way of life."

"Is chiding him the way to accomplish that?"

"We shall find out in time. What is the status of the city?"

"Burning, but they are slowly putting the fires out."

"Good. Now I have work to do Commander."

"Searcher, out."

Soraya went to her saddle bags and removed a leather roll, tapped it on her hand a couple of times then went to Roman's shelter. She wasn't looking for Roman, but she was wanting to talk with his teacher, Eli. Soraya found him sitting on a stool, drinking tea.

"Master Eli, I have a task for you."

He stood.

"Roman says you do not wish to be called anything except Soraya, yet you call me Master."

"You are an elder and one must respect our elders. Please, come and look at what I propose."

Eli smiled and nodded then followed her over to the table at the back of the shelter. She unrolled the leather to reveal several pieces of parchment. The parchments were simple drawing of a war machine.

"What is this Soraya?"

"It is called a Trebuchet. Do you understand the measurements?"

He bent over and looked closely at the drawing.

"Yes Soraya, I do. What is its purpose?"

"It is to sling large rocks, boulders over the city walls."

Eli looked up from the drawings and grinned.

"With this, Roman would not have to storm the wall of the city."

"No, he'll still have to fight to take it unless the people inside the walls surrenders the King. I have other things which need to be built, but this is a start. Gather your craftsmen and have them begin construction. Time is important and the more we expend in debate, the less we have in execution."

"I shall see to it now Soraya."

She turned away as he was rolling up the drawings.

"Soraya, may I ask a question of you?"

"Yes, you may."

"What is your purpose here?"

"To end this war and to help enlighten your people."

"You interest me Soraya. Last eve you turned down Roman when any number of females in the camp would have gone to his bed without pause. Your eyes are the color of grass in the early growing and your hair is that of grain ready to harvest, but those are not known here. You bring strange, new weapons with you that are unknown even to the King's army, yet you act as if you desire nothing from this. Roman does not desire to lead but it was placed upon him, and if he lives to see the end of this, he will be King, and the female at his side would be Queen."

"No Eli, Roman will never be King, but he could lead his people into a better life. I have no desire to be more than what I am, and at this time, I am the weapon he needs to fulfill his dreams of freedom for all people."

Eli nodded acceptance of her answer and finished rolling up the drawings as she left the shelter.

Soraya left the shelter and just walked through the camp, thinking about what had been said and what had to be done. Eli was right about Roman being able to find companionship and if it was not for the prophecy, she would even consider it, but at what risk to her and her future? Regardless of what had been foretold, she was still a woman and had been tempted more than once to surrender herself to a man.

She noticed as she walked and observed the cook fires that there was little meat to go with the meal. During their journey through the forest, she had seen many animals akin to what was once called an Elk, which was hunted for its meat. She turned back towards her camp with the thought of doing some hunting.

The men were nearly finished erecting a shelter based on the design Soraya had given them back at the camp. It was tall enough for any of her men to stand up in and open on one side so there would be no choke point in trying to exit it in an emergency. She smiled at seeing their bedrolls laid out, spaced out to give each person plenty of room to move around and using that as a guide to build the shelter.

"Derstin, Anton, do not forget to eat early so you can replace Steffen and Hammel at the gates. Take some trail meat with you and insure your water bladders are full. Porsett, get your bow and quiver, I think we need to take a couple animals for meat as it seems this camps larder is lacking in such."

They rode back up the trail from which they came until Soraya's AI told her there were several of the animals further off the trail into the woods. They dismounted, tying the horses to a bush, then with Soraya leading, they began to stalk the animals.

They came within twenty meters of the animals and it surprised Soraya they had not spooked them as Porsett was not light footed in the woods. Soraya drew back her bow and focused on where she wanted to place the arrow and released it. The animal bellowed, took four leaping steps then crashed to the ground. Her arrow had pierced the heart of the beast.

The animals that were near the one Soraya killed had ran a few meters then stopped, looked around for danger then went back to eating. Soraya whispered to Porsett to ease back to the horses and bring them back, so they would drag the huge beast out of the wood and onto the trail. As Porsett moved away, Soraya stalked a second animal and as with the first, it died quickly. The ability of the long bow arrow to penetrate deep in the animal made the kill better for the animal.

When Porsett returned, they tied the hind legs of the animals together then tied the rope to a horse and leading it out of the woods, drug the animals from the woods. One animal per horse. Soraya was not going to strain the horses in carrying them plus dragging the animal, so they just walked back to camp with Soraya in the lead and Porsett trailing since the rack of antlers on the animals were so large, they would not be able to walk side by side.

The pickets at the camp could not believe their eyes when Soraya walked past, dragging such a large animal behind her horse then Porsett dragging another. She was not sure on how they were going to butcher such a beast until Porsett told her he often did that on the farm when the master wanted the meat from a cow.

They found two large trees near where they were camped and Porsett threw another rope over a sturdy limb the tied it too the antlers. Once he was certain the rope was well tied, he used the horse to pull the animal into the air and into a position he could gut and skin the animal.

Porsett saw one of the Rebels watching him that was wearing a red armband and waved him over.

"Go find two more men and shovels so we can dig a hole to bury the innards of this animal."

"See this armband. I'm a leader, not a slave. Who are you to give me orders?" The man responded.

"I am an archer with Lady Soraya. She killed these beasts for meat and expects to have them for the evening meal."

"Oh, Lady Soraya. Yes, I'll find two men and some shovels."

By the time the man returned with two others and shovels, Porsett had the second animal hanging in a tree close to the first. He told the men to dig the hole between them and stay near as they would have to shovel the innards into the hole then cover it up.

Soraya set under the eve of their shelter and watched as Porsett with the help of the other men carefully skinned the large animals as she told him she desired the hides to be tanned for use as a cloak when the air turns cold.

She was sipping on a mug of spicy herbal tea when Roman walked to the edge of the shelter.

"Come Roman, sit and share my teapot."

She never looked his way as she spoke and was not wearing her helm. He just stood looking at her before speaking.

"Eli tells me you have him, and the wood craftsmen build a machine to throw large stones over the city walls."

"Yes, that is correct."

"You said that you would not take a place in this army, yet you are giving orders."

"Roman, please join me and let us talk about this in a peaceful manner."

Roman moved under the shelter's eve and sat down. Soraya handed him an empty mug, then picked up the pot from the edge of the fire and poured him some tea.

"Roman, you were not in your shelter when I went to see you, so I presented my idea to Eli knowing he would have to deal with it since your level of learning is not up to what I needed accomplished. It has nothing to do with me trying to take over your army, but to get what you need to finish this war quickly. Do you wish to challenge me to prove your manhood?"

Roman nearly choked on his tea when she spoke about a challenge.

"Soraya I may be uneducated, but I know better than to challenge one who carries a sword such as yours."

"Roman, intelligence has nothing to do with education, but the realization of ones weaknesses. It's not my sword you need to concern yourself with, but my ability to use it."

Roman did not speak as he sipped on the tea thinking about what she had said. It was several minutes later that a large rodent showed itself between them and the hole with the innards in it. It sat for a moment and in that time, Soraya drew the thin blade, a stiletto from her left arm and threw it at the rodent, hitting if just behind the front shoulder and driving through it's body. The rodent fell over, dead.

"Soraya, I know of no one that can do that. Are you a witch?"

"Some would say that Roman, but as I said, I came to help you, not to kill you. I shall do whatever I must to insure your victory. Once that is complete, I shall leave, never to return."

He looked out at the rodent again before replying.

"I shall tell my Lieutenants that you word will be obeyed."

"No Roman, obeyed is the wrong word. That makes them slaves again, and we must not have that if they are to be free."

"Then I will find a way to tell them without making it seem so. Do you have any other things we might use against the city?"

"Yes, I've been looking at it for some time now. See that large tree the beast Porsett is butchering is hanging from? Find another like it, have it cut down and trimmed. We need the body of the tree intact and laid upon a flat wagon. I'll explain it all better once the tree is ready for the wagon. Understand?"

"May I ask the purpose of the tree?"

"Yes, to open the city gates."

Roman called to one of the men that was watching the butchering. When the man came to him, Roman repeated to him what Soraya told him. The man looked at the tree, nodded then left to find another like that one and others to help him in his task.

When Steffen and Hammel returned after being relieved, Steffen told of twelve guards that came through the gates at them with lances ready to do battle. Steffen said they killed seven of them before the others turned back to the gates. Hammel commented they did not fire upon those fleeing back into the city. Later, with Steffen covering him, Hammel went to the dead and stripped them of weapons and other items they might need.

Once that was accomplished, Steffen called to the guards out of sight on the wall and told them to come collect their dead, and they could do so without fear of harm as long as they made no attempt to attack them. It was some time before the gates opened and unarmed men came out and drug the dead back into the city.

That night the stew pots has chunks of meat in them and Soraya and her archers ate large steaks.

Soraya kept a rotation of archers at the gates including standing a watch with them that night. The men on the wall learned soon after she arrived to remove any torch or type of light behind

46

them after she killed two more men. This didn't matter to her as she could still see them even without the aid of her helm, but let the men on the wall believe for now that they were safe without a torch or candle.

Improvements

When Soraya returned after daylight to the camp, she gave Eli further instructions with Roman standing by observing. This time it wasn't instructions on building a weapon, but latrines for sanitation, and pits to dispose of waste food. She had to explain that if these things were not done, soon Roman's army would become sick from disease which would cripple his ability to fight the King.

Since very few of the men and women could read, she had pieces of red cloth hung on latrines for the women and brown for the men. The word was passed to the people to only use the one colored for them, so the females would have privacy in the act.

Trent and the wagons from the farm arrived mid-morning. He apologized for not arriving sooner, but one wagon lost a wheel and it took time to repair. Soraya told him that no one faulted him because of an unforeseen accident.

She gathered her craftsmen together and found a place for them to work out of view of the city, and had Eli bring Roman's craftsmen to join with them as they continued making the long bow and arrows needed for archers. Her weaver took ten women in hand and taught them how the strings for the bows were to be made and set about weaving the strings with Soraya telling them that extra strings per man would be a good idea just in case one broke due to bad material, not poor craftsman ship.

With the arrival of the wagons her force of archers grew to sixty-one and she had them set up targets for practice. Soon, others from Roman's army joined to learn how to use a bow with Roman standing in the front of them as a student.

To many it seemed that Soraya never slept more than an hour or two as she seemed to be everywhere providing guidance in the bow training or the construction of implements of war. Crude forges were built, and metal was worked into arms for the men and knives for the women. Soraya showed how if a hot blade was

48

placed in the petroleum which seeped from the ground it would make the steel harder, less brittle when struck by other steel.

She had the camps surrounding the city stripped of all but ten men per camp with instructions they were to be seen milling about during the day and to keep fires lit at night to remind those in the city they were surrounded.

The men she brought into the main camp, she had move back into the forest, so they would not be seen if the people in the city had seeing lenses, telescopes, in which to watch them. Soraya had to keep much of her speech simple for these people to understand her concepts, but they caught on quickly as she built a real army.

Soraya returned to the gates with all of her archers, three days after Trent and the wagons arrived and called for someone on the wall to speak with her with the promise they would not be harmed if they exposed themselves. She told the man who was brave enough to stand where she could see him that she was pulling her archers from the gates, but if a single body was seen hanging, they would return and once more set the city on fire.

Upon return to the camp, Soraya sent twenty of her archers along with Trent back to the farm to gather more grain and food for the army. Word had came to them there was another farm to the West that was still in the hands of the King's men and she sent Steffen with another twenty archers to liberate that farm with instructions to return with their wagons as full as possible with food and of course, all of the freed slaves.

Roman and his Lieutenants were becoming impatient as they wanted to take the city, but Soraya told them that in time, food would become scare within the city and once the rock throwers were complete and tested, they would give the people in the city reason to open the gates without having to use the ram they had constructed.

Time was on the side of the people who had the food, not the people who were locked in the city, unable to obtain it.

She had wooden swords made and watched Roman and his Lieutenants fight with them for several hours before she took over instruction, teaching them how to use them with less expenditure of energy. She took them step by step, showing the men how to slash and block, then once she was confident they understood the basics, she sent them out to train their own men.

Soraya explained to them that they had been lucky as the King's army did not understand who they were fighting but now, given time, they would be better prepared and in doing so, would greatly diminish the Rebel army. She proved that by taking on five men at once, defeating them all in a matter of minutes with her skills with a blade. Soraya held back her true abilities to prove a point that even a lesser man could defeat them if they were trained.

Days turned into weeks as she trained Roman's army. When the Trebuchet was finished, they tested it using different weights in the counter-weight until she felt they had a good balance, then she had the Trebuchet disassembled and the parts carried to a point outside of the city to be reassembled. As it was being reassembled, she had archers and men armed with lances and swords guarding the workers in case the King's army sallied from the gates.

Wagons brought stones of various sizes to the location and once everything was in position and ready, they waited until the sun was high in the sky to launch the first stone. It sailed high over the walls and a crashing sound could be heard from the city as it tore through the wooded roof of a house or building.

She had different weight stones placed into the sling, allowing each toss to go further or shorter and after two hours, she ceased firing on the city. Cries and screams could be heard over the walls but what Roman and his men did not know was Soraya was getting a bird's eye view of what was happening inside the walls.

The Searcher was cloaked and down in the atmosphere over the city and relaying video of the panic inside the city. It was using that video that she selected each stone to be thrown. The range depended on weight, the accuracy depended upon how the stone was placed in the sling and shape of the stone. She wanted range over accuracy as she was finally able to hit the Palace, giving notice to the King he was not immune from the violence.

Her last act before leaving the city, was to have a dozen of her archers fire messages tied to arrows which she had Eli write, advising the citizens of the city they could leave, with only the possessions they could carry and if they had any slaves, they were to release them to her archers once outside of the city. The citizens would be taken to a farm where there was food and shown how to harvest the crops growing there.

The guards at the Trebuchet reported loud noises from inside the wall hours after the arrows went over the wall which Soraya knew was rioting by the citizens against troops as they tried to leave the city.

This set the stage for the next step in her plan.

For the past week, Soraya had twenty men pushing the ram wagon up and down the trail to the camp out of sight of the city, learning how to push it and keep it going in the right direction. At midnight, they slowly moved the ram to the road leading to the city gates then the men walked the road, using their feet to find any large stone which might cause the wagon to deflect from the path intended for it.

To help during the run on the gate, Soraya had unlit torches placed along the final fifty meters to the gates. At the right time, two of her archers would light the torches to provide a guide for the men handling the ram.

She gathered her forces one last time to remind them of her orders. No person leaving the city will be harmed as long as they lay down their arms. She drew her scimitar to express what would happen to anyone violating her orders. Anyone wanting to leave would be given the chance and warned to drop their arms. But each warning had to be loud and clear in meaning.

When they first brought the ram into position, the guards on the wall could not see what was happening since the two moons were in wane and over the horizon. Fearing attack by the archers, the guards moved off the wall, so they did not see when the torches were lit to guide the ram into the gate. Soraya did put two archers on either side of the road in case a guard got brave and attempted to throw a lance at the men pushing the ram.

Before she ordered the ram to attack the gate, Soraya had the Trebuchet fire several stones over the walls to distract the guards even more. She had baskets of small stones, slightly larger than a man's fist fired over the wall which dispersed the small stones in extremely random patterns, injuring several men who were moving about the city, trying to help those injured or displaced from their homes by the stones.

The men began pushing the wagon as the archers ran down the road to light the torches building momentum as he wagon moved forward. Soraya and Roman were standing to the side of the gate as they approached and when she knew the wagon was going to hit the gate squarely, she yelled for the men to get away from it.

Soraya had studied the sensor data on the gate and knew that a ram one fourth of the weight of this one would penetrate the wooden gate, but she wanted to set the stage for her entrance. On impact with the ram, the gate shattered, sending chunks of wood everywhere as the wagon continued into the city, finally coming to rest against a fountain in the city square approximately eighty meters inside the walls.

The wagon was still moving when Soraya told Roman to stay outside the gate, then followed it into the city, stopping about twenty meters inside gate and just stood looking around until danger came at her from her left side. A sentry with a lance came at her, but she pivoted away from the lance head, drawing her scimitar as she spun and slicing the sentry's body in two pieces as her scimitar completed the arch.

The screams of the sentry did not last long as shock overrode his ability to utter a sound seconds before death took him. Soraya never looked down at the body, only around her as she stood waiting. No one else challenged her.

"Who is in charge here? Bring him forth so I may speak with him!" Her voice was enhanced by the AI in her helm.

A man stepped forward from a group that was standing to her right front.

"I am the Captain of the Guard." He spoke.

"Come forward then Captain and listen well to what I have to say."

The men moved about half the distance from Soraya and stopped. He had witnessed the death of one of his men but the person who did it was unlike anyone he had ever seen before even if she was a female. Soraya had dressed Centaurian style with a black halter, black calf high boots except that instead of wearing a thong, she was wearing low cut black panties.

From this view point, the Captain could see daggers extending from the boots, and what appeared to be one strapped to her left arm. The glossy black leather against her white body in the light of torches looked both erotic yet announced the danger this female possessed. And the real danger was the glowing, green sword she held in her right hand. It had cut through his sentry like a blade through smoke, and it seemed as if it was on fire as she held it pointed at the ground.

"Speak witch."

Soraya laughed.

"Heed me well Captain. The gates of your city are now open, and they shall stay open. Let it be known that in four days, if the King is not surrendered to me, I will once more enter this city and when I leave, no man or woman will be left alive. Until then, any citizen that wishes to leave may do so without arms and once any slave or servant passes through the open gate, they are free from bondage, free to live as they decide. Do you understand my words Captain?"

"Yes, I hear and understand your words, witch."

Soraya pointed her sword at the captain again.

"Do not depend on others to spread my word to the people as I now hold you responsible for telling others what I have spoken this night."

She flipped her scimitar and returned it to its scabbard, then reached into the small pouch in the middle of her back and removed a pencil flare that was part of the aviator's survival kit. She palmed it in her right hand, then pointed at the ram wagon. The ram and wagon had been soaked in crude petroleum and when she activated the flare, it seemed as if fire erupted from her fingers and traveled to the wagon which immediately caught fire.

Soraya turned back towards the gate laughing with her helm amplifying her voice. If they were going to call her a witch, let them think so. She walked through the gates and mounted her horse that Steffen was holding for her. They rode back to a safe distance before stopping and looking at the burning ram and wagon.

"Steffen, you know my words about dealing with anyone who wishes to leave the city. See that no one violates those words."

"Yes Soraya."

She reined her horse over and headed to the camp only to meet Roman who was sitting on his horse away from the rest of the men.

"Four days Roman, I gave them four days and if they do not turn the King over to you, then you do as you wish with the city. The gates are open now and my archers will see that it stays open."

"Soraya, you are a witch. I saw the fire come from your fingers to set the wagon on fire."

"No Roman, that is science. Technology far above this world."

"This world? Where do you come from Soraya?"

"From far away Roman. A place you will never see, but in time those from your loins may see that place."

She left Roman thinking about her words and not understanding half of them.

After a few hours sleep, Soraya decided she needed a bath. After she had latrines set up, she noticed that the only place to bath was the stream where they drew their water. But being wide open, the men would watch the females and often make comments to and about them as they bathed, plus the point they bathed was up stream were most drew their water.

Soraya had screens built and the locations marked for male or female bathing and she convinced Roman to issue instructions concerning a male entering the females area and what could happen to them.

She took the things she needed to the nearest female bathing area and entered seeing there were a few females also bathing. Soraya laid her things out and stripped. Along the bank of the area were stools she could take into the stream and sit on as she washed the dirt and sweat from her body.

The females there were using a homemade soap while she was using one of the non-fragrance soap bars from a survival kit. Just as she was lathering her breasts one of the females already in the stream came over to her.

"Lady Soraya, may I ask you a question?"

Soraya looked at the female. Her breasts had lost their firmness of youth and from the stretch marks on her abdomen, she had experienced childbirth.

"My name is only Soraya, not Lady Soraya. What is your name?"

"Anais. My name is Anais."

"Yes Anais, you may ask me a question."

"Soraya, it is known within the camp you do not share your bed with a man even though you sleep under a shelter with your men. Is it because you prefer a female?"

Soraya could only smile at Anais as she suspected what was on her mind before answering.

"Anais, I am untouched by man and female. I have no desire to bed another female and the man I search for to bed me is one that is not within this camp. Why do you ask?"

"Soraya, there are some of us females that enjoy another female from time to time, and a place such as this is a good place to have that enjoyment since the men cannot watch us."

"Explain this to me Anais."

"Before the selection, the overseers made us females they were guarding bed another female as they watched and often made themselves expend their seed on the ground as they watched. They said it was to prepare us for selection and after selection, they made us once more take a female as part of preparing us to be violated by them. Some females only did it because of fear of the overseers while others, myself included, found pleasure in such acts. Once we were turned out to work in the quarry, if we wanted to enjoy another female, we had to endure the men watching us and often once we were finished, the men would take us where we lay."

"How many children have you born?"

"Four, but only three lived to grow. My first was given to me by an overseer, the others by men in the quarry."

"Did Roman use your body?"

"Yes, before he was taken to the Palace, but when he returned, he only took a female that offered herself."

"Do you know who fathered your children?"

"No Soraya, many men used me between births and any man could be the father of any of my children although one does have Roman's look."

"How old are you Anais? Or do you know?"

"It is said I am twenty-four annuals."

Soraya looked at Anais thinking she looked to be in her mid-thirties. Even as hard as life had been on her, she was still modestly attractive. With having four children, the hard work in the quarry had melted away the fat that women gain during pregnancy.

"Are you offering yourself to me Anais?"

"Yes Soraya. I can think of several pleasures with you."

"Thank you, Anais, but no, I will not lay with you. If I would lay with another female, you would be one I would consider."

"Then I shall leave you to your bath Soraya. If I offended you, forgive me."

"I am not offended, in fact I take your words as a compliment. May the day bring you happiness."

"And to you also Soraya."

Soraya finished bathing and when she moved back up the bank to dry and put on her linens, she noticed off in a corner, where it was shaded, the bodies of two females in the act of making love to one another. She just turned away to give them that privacy and never considered if Anais might be one of them.

As she walked back to her shelter, she thought DNA testing could either bring families together or cause a great rift amongst the former slaves. The men unsure who sired the many children running around the camp treated all of them as if they were their own children.

Parentage

At this point, there was nothing for Soraya to do except wait out the time she had allowed the people of the city to respond to her ultimatum. Deep inside she felt that it would end with violence even though she was wishing for peace.

It had been two days since she had stood inside the city gates and Steffen had been sending back reports every few hours of people leaving the city without any problems from either side. She hated having to disarm the people leaving the city, but she was not going to have armed men to the rear of the Rebels.

All people escaping the city were told to travel down the road for approximately twenty leagues to a farm where they would find food and some shelter. Soraya had convinced Roman to put some of the older men and women from his army there to assist those people and to protect them from danger. The rule concerning molesting any male or female in the people arriving there was the same as when they left the city.

The number of freed slaves and servants increased the population of the Rebel encampment and Soraya's archers went deep into the forest to harvest animals for meat. She warned her hunters to be careful not to completely destroy the animal population as they would need to have them repopulate the forest for later generations.

Soraya was resting, just laid back against the wall of her shelter dressed in a simple coverlet like many of the women wore with her black synthetic halter and panties beneath. She could change into her leathers in seconds if need be and her sword was always within arm's reach.

There was a commotion from Roman's shelter and she rose up to see one of his men standing in front of it and pointing towards the city. She had to stand and look in that direction to see a rider coming at a gallop. Soraya stepped into her shelter and quickly changed.

Soraya came out of her shelter ready to fight if necessary as the rider was leaned over in his saddle talking to Roman. Roman laughed then looked over at Soraya as she was walking towards him. He waited until she was within arm's reach before speaking.

"Soraya, there is a female that says she is the Queen outside the gate with her maids wanting to talk to me. Care to ride?"

"Certainly, I'd like to meet this woman."

Soraya turned back to her shelter to see Porsett astride his horse with Soraya's horses reigns in his hand. He kept a horse saddled for her around the clock in case she had to go into battle in a rush. All she had to do was tighten the saddle before mounting the horse. Her bow and quiver was always ready, attached to the saddle for easy reach.

No one spoke as they rode to the checkpoint where the female wishing to see Roman was waiting, but as they closed the distance, Soraya could see that the individual was waiting in a nicely adorned open carriage with attendants.

When they closed with the carriage, a female is fine clothing stood, assisted by the other females in the carriage. There was no mistaken that she was with child and looking at the maids, they were also with child. They female spoke first.

"Roman, I come to ask for sanctuary for myself and my maids in your house."

"In my house? Queen Reita, why my house? Once you left the city your maids were free to live as they wish without you."

"Roman, it is because the spawn I carry inside of me, and my maids carry inside of them are yours."

"Mine? What manner of deception are you attempting to place upon me?"

"No deception Roman. The King is incapable of producing a single child and if you remember, my maids were virgin when you

59

took them in your quarters while you were in the city working the keystone."

Soraya carefully mutter commands to her AI who scanned the Queen then reported what it detected.

"Soraya, the female is with twins." The AI advised.

Soraya only smiled at that knowledge then spoke to Reita.

"How can you prove the spawn you carry is Roman's?"

"Witch, go to Harold's harem. Of the females there you will find that none of them are with child."

Soraya dismounted and walked to the Queen, quietly giving her AI instructions. When Soraya raised her hand, the Queen started to move back from Soraya.

"Stand easy Reita, I only wish to touch your swollen belly."

As Soraya was gently holding her hand against Reita's belly, her AI was looking deep into it at the children she carried, sorting out the infants DNA from their mother and comparing it to Roman's DNA which it had stored in its memory. Soon it had an answer and gave it to Soraya through her earpiece. Soraya laughed then turned to Roman.

"Roman, they are your spawn. Twins, a boy and a girl."

Roman had a stunned look on his face.

"Soraya, how can you say they are mine and there are twins growing inside of her."

Soraya never answered as she turned back to the Queen.

"Why did you take Roman to your bed if you knew he could give you a child?"

"Because if it was a male child, I would have arranged for Harold to meet with an accident and became regent until our son

60

was of age to take the throne. Roman, I do not like how females are treated any more than you. The blood line to the throne passes through me, not Harold as I am the daughter of King Morsette. I had no choice as my marriage to Harold was arranged by my father. I hoped that as the child grew, I could teach him to be gentler and to change the way we live."

Roman stepped off his horse and walked up to her.

"And your maids, what of them? Did you send them to my bed?"

"Yes Roman, because if the child you gave me was female, then I prayed to the Gods that one of them would have a male child and I would exchange one for the other."

"Reita, you said you did not like the way females were treated yet you had one prepare you for our mating, then had your maids clean us. That does not speak of one who does not like how females are treated. And to have them impregnated by me so you could have a male child to replace Harold."

"Roman, the females are known to me as they are to each other. Each one agreed to play the part they played those nights, so it would seem normal to you. They knew of my plan to remove Harold."

"What of Harold?" Soraya asked.

"Witch, the city is yours for the taking. The guards are loyal to me, and I ordered them to lay down their arms and allow you to enter the city, and the palace. You will probably find Harold in his harem buggering one of his young boys as he seems to favor them over the females."

Soraya turned to Steffen.

"Steffen gather four men and go to the Palace. Do not enter, but tell the guards to bring Harold to Roman here outside the gate. Tell them if Harold is not here when the sun is on the horizon, I

61

shall enter and end their miserable lives before removing Harold myself. Go, be quick and safe."

"Yes Soraya."

Steffen indicated four other archers and with their bows in hand and swords on their hips, they went into the city.

"What now Soraya?" Roman asked.

"Roman, it is time for the men to accept their place as father's. Before you is the results of your lust. Now you must pay the price for such action. But the last thing this world needs is another King. I shall teach you and the others a set of Principles which can lead your world to enlightenment."

"Soraya, I never wanted to be a King or even lead this revolt, but I have tried to lead well."

"You have done well Roman, but to be free also means being able to choose your leaders. You may lead still, but never as King even if you bond with Reita once we arrange Harold's fatal divorce."

Roman looked up at Reita as she still stood in the carriage.

"I think I understand your words Soraya. Is Reita free to accept or refuse bonding with me?"

"Of course, she is, as are her maids which also carry your spawn, but if you wish to find honor, you may find yourself with a very large family and numerous wives."

Porsett laughed from hearing what Soraya said. Roman turned to look at him.

"Porsett, why are you laughing?"

"Roman, with that many wives you once again become a slave, but this time to their desires."

Roman just shook his head then turned to Soraya who was smiling before looking up at Reita. But when he spoke, he spoke to Porsett.

"Porsett, take Reita and her maids to my shelter and make them comfortable. Please ask Eli to see to their needs until we return so we can talk about this more."

"Certainly Roman."

Reita sat back down, then her carriage driver turned the horses towards the camp and followed Porsett, who rode slightly ahead of them.

Roman looked at Soraya.

"What do we do now?"

"We wait, Roman. We wait."

Reunion

It was almost an hour before Steffen returned with what appeared to be a guard behind them nearly dragging a small man who was dressed in a sleeping gown out of the gate. Soraya began feeling a tingling in her body even before she was able to get a clear look at those following Steffen and his men, and the closer they came, the tingling intensified. Steffen never said a word as he moved to the side of Soraya and Roman.

The guard stopped back from Soraya and Roman, then slung the little man down at their feet, then spoke.

"I give you King Harold of Phaedra."

Soraya was all but shaking as if in a bitter winter wind as she looked at the guard. He was as tall, with coal black hair and a light beard. His heavy brows rested over eyes so dark they looked black. When he spoke, his voice was deep, but it seemed to pierce Soraya's ability to control herself. He started to turn back to the city when Soraya stopped him.

"Wait, your name sir?"

He turned back to her and spoke.

"Linus, My Lady."

"Do you know who I am Linus?"

"Yes, My Lady, you are Soraya, the one all call a witch."

Soraya looked down at Harold who was groveling in the dirt as he was whimpering in fear. As she stepped forward to Harold she drew her scimitar, jabbed Harold in the side causing him to jerk and extend his neck, and in a single, swift movement, Soraya removed his head with a single strike to the neck. She then kneeled down and wiped the edge of her sword on the hem on his gown before standing back up and looking at Roman.

"Roman, you are now free to take the city, and Reita as your wife without anyone claiming you killed Harold to have her."

No one spoke as Harold's blood soaked the ground. Soraya turned to Steffen.

"Steffen, have the men gather wood and pile it here next to Harold, place his body and head on it and tend to the fire until nothing exists of his body, then spread the ashes across the fields."

"It will be done Soraya."

She then turned to Linus.

"So, this world in called Phaedra?"

He gave her an odd look then smiled.

"Yes, My Lady, it is. This is not known to you?"

"I come from far away where the name is unknown."

"As you say My Lady."

She turned to Anton.

"Anton, find Linus a horse." Turning to Linus. "Attend me please we have things to do before the day turns to night."

"I am not a slave My Lady to be ordered about in such a manner now that my master lies without his head."

"No Linus you are not, but what we do this day needs to be known to those still in the city and I cannot think of a better way to ensure they receive that word but from you."

Soraya still had her sword in hand and flipped it, then laid it across her bent arm, offering him its grip. He paused for a second then took it in hand, raised it up and looked at the green glow of the engraving and edge of the blade before returning it too Soraya. She accepted the sword and returned it too its scabbard.

"Yes, My Lady, I will go with you."

Soraya was struggling to control her emotions as Linus was the one she had been searching for all of her adult life. If he had not been, the sword would have burnt his hand due to the spell upon it. She mounted her horse and waited until Porsett brought one up for Linus who adjusted the stirrups before mounting up.

When they arrived at the camp, Soraya instructed Eli to gather all of the scholars and insure there was plenty of parchment and writing instruments. She took Linus to her shelter and offered him tea as they waited for Eli and the others.

Roman went to Reita and told her about Harold's demise and that she was now free to determine her own life. She looked around his humble shelter before commenting.

"Roman, I will stay with you if you will have me even if I must live like this, and learn how to tend to your needs without maids to assist me."

"Why Reita? Do you love me?"

"No Roman, maybe in time, but a child needs a father and I know what it is like not to have one as other children did. Since I was female, my father ignored me, used me when it benefited him then gave me to a man who would take his place on the throne for reasons I never learned."

"And your maids?"

"Their lives are theirs to live. If you wish them also, I shall not stand between you and them. But once I give birth to your children, I would expect nights with you as what brought me to this condition."

He looked around the shelter then shook his head.

"Soraya is correct that I must act with honor. I created this problem and must act with honor on it. This shelter is not big enough for all of us, so we must find another place for all of us."

"Roman, the palace is mine until you decide otherwise. There is plenty of room for us there in my former chambers without you taking the throne unless you desire that too."

"No, Soraya says I must never take the throne, and I have learned not to doubt her thoughts."

"Roman, where is the witch from?"

"Reita, she says she is from the Northern mountains, and if she is indeed a witch, then I am thankful she is with me instead of against me."

"So, she also shares your bed?"

"No Reita, she shares no man's or woman's bed. She is a strange one."

At the same time, Linus was observing Soraya as she waited for Eli to return.

"Lady Soraya, why are you so nervous? I mean you no harm."

"Linus, please do not call my Lady Soraya. I am only Soraya."

"Certainly Soraya. May I speak openly to you?"

"You may."

"I sense you are fighting your emotions. Why is that?"

Soraya looked at Linus and knew it was a mistake bringing him back to her shelter, but she had to answer his question with complete honesty. Before she could find the words, she needed to say, Eli entered the shelter with three other men rescuing her from the moment.

Over the next two hours she quoted the Principles of Leadership which governed the Federation from memory, taking time for each scholar to carefully write the words down. During a pause, she looked at Linus.

"Linus, can you read?"

"Yes Soraya, I wouldn't be much of a senior guard if I could not."

"Very good as you need to see a copy of these Principles are scribed in the Palace and given to the city people to learn."

"I understand and thank you for your trust."

She just nodded to him and continued to dictate the Principles. Once finished she looked at each parchment to ensure they were exactly as dictated and readable before handing Linus one copy.

"Linus take this to the palace scribes and have them make others for the people. I place it upon you to ensure they do not deviate from the wording, and those that cannot read, have people to read these words to them."

He slightly bowed to her as he took the parchment. As he did so, he took her hand in his then bent over and lightly kissed it. Soraya nearly came apart at his touch.

"Why did you do that?" She asked.

"Because I desired to do so."

"Go Linus, and do what I have asked of you."

He started to turn then looked back at her.

"We are not done you and I, but I shall wait for you."

As he rode back to the city, Soraya watched him against the background of the smoke from Harold's funeral fire. Her hand where he kissed it felt odd and she looked at it and panicked. The spot were his lips touched her hand had turned a pale blue. She closed her eyes and focused on her hand then when she looked back at it, it was once again normal.

Yes, she thought, he was the one. But did he know how this would end between them?

She returned to her shelter, retrieved her helm and walked out into the open terrain towards the city. As she was walking away from the camp she activated her personal cloaking device in the pouch on her left hip. Anyone watching would have seen her disappear in the blink of an eye.

"Searcher, this is Soraya, over."

"This is Searcher, go ahead Soraya, over."

"Searcher, please send down the survey ship cloaked, please. I need to file my report, over."

"Stand by your location Soraya, this will take a few minutes, over."

"Standing by, over."

It was nearly thirty minutes later that her helm advised her the survey ship was approaching and lowered the built in visor, so she could see the ship in its cloaked condition. The ship landed and once settled on its skids, the cockpit canopy opened to allow her to enter. She strapped in and told the ships AI to return to the Searcher.

Once it was safe to leave the survey ship, Soraya left her scimitar and her helm in the ship's seat before entering the ship itself. Her cloaking device had an automatic shut-off when she entered the ship which made her seem to pop into the main cabin.

Before she began making her report, she went to her locker and removed her light robe, then stripped naked, placed her clothes into the refresher, then stepped into the small sanitary facilities and cleansed her body. Once clean she dawned her robe and stepped out to come face to face with Hank, the Searcher's commander.

"Soraya, what were you thinking when you took the King's head?"

"My thinking was and is that if Roman is to bond with Queen Reita, he cannot be held accountable for Harold's death. He had no say-so in the execution and can honestly make that claim as there were witnesses to our conversations up to that point. He is going to have enough problems forming a government as it is, he doesn't need that trouble."

"Will that be in your field report?"

"Certainly, if you think it should be included."

"I do. Soraya this had to be a rough assignment for you. Are you alright?"

"Commander Dodge, I see the end of my mission is near, but there is still things to do before I can abandon this world and leave it to Federation diplomats to sort the wheat from the chaff."

Dodge did not reply as she walked past him to a work station and began her report. It took over an hour before she finalized the report and transmitted it to the Fleet Sector Command. She changed back into her now clean clothing and without speaking to any of the crew, she hung her robe back into her locker, then removed a sealed bag from the bottom of the locker before returning to the survey ship for the return to the planet.

When she exited the survey ship, she stood looking towards the camp to make sure no one was watching before she turned off her cloak to reappear. She walked back to her shelter and mounted her horse. Porsett jumped up from his pad and started for his own horse.

"Porsett, stay and rest. I'm going to the city and what I have to do I must do alone. I shall return tomorrow and hopefully we can finish what Roman started."

Porsett just nodded and watched as she rode off towards the city.

70

When she passed the checkpoint, they were still adding wood to the funeral fire, but the stench of burning flesh was no longer in the air. Soraya passed through the gate to see workers cleaning up the remains of the burned ram and scrubbing the soot from the fountain stones. No one seemed to pay her any attention as she slowly rode through the city to the palace.

Soraya dismounted at the palace steps and tied her mare to an ornate post, then removed the saddle from the horse, placing it out of the way. With her package in hand, she went up the steps to the open palace doors and stopped before entering, turning to a guard to speak.

"Guard see that my horse is fed and watered, while I am in the palace. I do not know when I shall leave but I do not wish to see that the mare is wanting. Make sure your relief understands this or I will remove fingers from those who do not fulfill my wishes."

"Yes, My Lady." Was the response which had a hint of fear in the voice.

She turned to the other guard.

"Take me to the Queen's chambers."

"Yes, My Lady."

At the Queen's quarters, the guard opened the door for her then stood aside. Soraya looked to see the only light in the quarters came through two stained glass windows. She turned back to the guard.

"Thank you for your guidance, now I have one further task for you. Go find the guard named Linus. He should be with the palace scribes and advise him where I am and tell him I wish to speak to him. Be quick about it as time is important."

"Yes, My Lady"

Soraya entered the chambers, leaving the door open and snapped her fingers. Every candle in the chambers lit, providing light for her to examine the room. She had to laugh as the bed was large enough for several people. As she moved towards what she guessed was the Queen's dressing room, she waved her hand and the bed covers moved back to allow a person to lie upon it.

She entered the dressing room and laid her package off to the side on a table, then removed her helm, away from the package. Next came her scimitar which she laid next to the helm. When she took her vest off, she laid it over the helm to insure the optics did not record what was to happen within the room.

Soraya stripped of all her clothing and weapons then using the stiletto she wore on her left forearm, she cut the seal on the package, returned the stiletto to its sheath, and carefully opened the package.

Lying on top was a gossamer thin gown which she carefully removed, shook it once then put it on, tying it closed at her navel. Next came a small, velvet bag from which she removed a crystal tear-drop medallion hanging from a delicate silver chain. She kissed the medallion before putting it around her neck.

In another velvet bag she removed a gold wrist band and snapped in around her left wrist. It immediately seemed to tighten on her wrist as she reached for the last velvet bag from which she removed a silver wrist band and placed it on her right wrist. It too shrunk to fit snug. Both bands were engraved with marking which had not been seen anywhere in the universe except old Earth in the times of knights and kings.

The last item in her package was a jewel encrusted gold hair brush. Her hair had grown below her shoulders but as she brushed her hair, it seemed to lengthen with each stroke until it was near her waist.

Soraya smiled as she heard hobnailed boots on the floor stones in the hallway becoming louder as the wearer came closer until she heard them enter the chambers. A voice came as the footsteps stopped.

"Soraya are you here?"

"Yes, Linus, I shall only be a moment. Close the door please so no one can hear us speak to one another."

Soraya heard the door close then Linus move further into the room. She took a deep breath to try to claim her nerves, then laid the brush down as she turned for the door to the dressing room. With each step she could feel butterflies fluttering in her stomach.

She left the dressing room and took two steps before stopping, looking at Linus who was returning her gaze. There was no hiding her form in the gown she was wearing.

"Soraya, you are beautiful, but is this what is to be this day?"

"Linus, yes, this is what is to be this day, but first we have a small detail to attend too before that can happen."

"What is that Soraya?"

She walked to him as she carefully withdrew the medallion from between her breasts. It was hot in her hand and the heat did not come from the closeness of her body to it. Soraya stopped just inside arms reach of Linus and extended the medallion to Linus.

"Take it in your hands Linus."

Soraya could see his desire for her in his eyes as he carefully reach out and took the medallion from her hand. The effect was almost immediate as his hand clinched around it. He began to shake as if he had grabbed a live wire, then his head moved back as if looking at the ceiling and from deep inside of him came a sound that penetrated the walls of the chamber and resonated throughout the palace. It was the sound like that of an animal howling at the moon.

He finally released the medallion, but the effect was still coursing through his body as Soraya took several steps back from him and watched as his body slowly calmed, and his scream subsided.

His head drooped to his chest for a moment before looking back to view Soraya.

"Soraya, what have you done to me?"

Soraya smiled as she raised her arms over her head then brought the two wrist bands together causing a shimmering glow to surround her from the tips of her fingers to the floor. Linus watched as she transformed.

Her skin turned a pale blue in a wave starting at her hands to complete the change at her bare feet. The gold of her hair changed from the look of grain stalks to the of spun gold as it shined with a brilliance. Her lips darkened to a deep blue as did her nipples exposed through the gown. As this was happening, her ears transformed. Lengthening upwards to a point.

Linus smiled as he watched her change. Her body and face was still that of Soraya, but the rest told him of a long, lost memory.

"Gia?"

"Yes Cyril, it is I, Gia. I have came for you to return you to our home world."

"What has happened to me? I have memories I do not remember taking part in."

"Cyril, this was your punishment for disobeying the Council. You have lived a hundred lives since your exile from Delphi, as you were born and died only to be reborn again. All those memories are now within you, both good and bad. I have lived but one life as I waited for the Council to pardon you, so you could return to take your place before the Council."

"How long has it been since my lips touched yours?"

"Over a thousand years and in that time no other has touched my lips and my body is still untouched by another. We still have much to do as normal humans on this world, but until the morrow, I am yours as I once promised."

74

She untied the gown and let it slip off her shoulders.

There was a twinkle in his eyes as he looked at her yet pointed to the door and moved his hand. The sound of the bolts sliding into place, locking the door made her laugh as the old Cyril was back in her life. As he stepped towards her, he began to transform as his ears elongated and his clothes seemed to fall off his body exposing black fur covering his entire body. When he was in reach of her, she stopped him with a clawed finger of a raptor in his chest.

"Cyril, take me as a normal human, or as you truly are, but we are too old to be playing werewolf and maiden, and I'll have you no other way."

He stood with her claw sticking him in his chest and once more transformed into his former appearance except his skin tone was a darker blue than hers and his eyes were gold in color as his hair turned a deep blue.

"Now there is the man I fell in love with." She spoke as her clawed hand returned to human form. "Never attempt to take me any other way Cyril as you know I can make you suffer for upsetting me."

He laughed as he reached out and pulled her to him and they kissed, holding each other tight. When they broke the kiss, he picked her up and carried her to the bed to finally consummate their love.

Discovery

When Cyril/Linus awoke he found himself alone in bed. He moaned as he rolled over and sat up after a long night of passion with a woman who seemed she could not be satisfied. Looking towards the dressing room he saw Soraya standing in the door of the room smiling at him. Gia had returned to her Soraya persona and was dressed accordingly, leaving her jerkin on the table covering her helm.

"Damn woman, I think you have ruined me."

"Stop complaining my Love, as it seemed you had no problem fulfilling my desires last night, and the only reason I am able to stand is that Soraya was not damaged by your passion as Gia was. I had to transform before I could even get out of bed. Now change back to Linus as we have much to do today."

Cyril transformed and then stretched before moving off the bed. He worked his back some as if getting kinks out of it before making a motion with his left hand causing his clothes to return to his body. Soraya laughed.

"Laugh all you want woman, but even Linus is aching from last night. Now what are your plans My Lady Soraya?"

"We break our fast then there are a couple questions the Federation have no answers too."

They had talked during the short breaks of lust during the night which Soraya explained what the Federation was and what they were doing in this part of space.

"What questions are those Soraya?"

"The first question is what are humans doing in this part of space and how did they get here? The DNA samples I was able to take during my survey shows the humans here are unaltered Earth humans. Then the other question is the state of the population in its medieval form. One may indicate the other."

76

He stood for a long time as if searching his memory of his previous lives.

"Soraya, there is nothing in my memory that says this world has been any different as you found it. Whatever stunted its growth happened before the Council exiled me to this world. Soraya, I have done things in other lives that shame me."

Soraya walked to him and put her fingers to his lips.

"Cyril, put those things aside and use them to guide you to a better place. I too have done things even in this current form which could cause me to stand before the Council in shame, but I had to do them in order to move the path of this world to a better place without the survivors living in guilt for their actions. Now let us go find the kitchen and refresh ourselves."

He took her hand and kissed it before pulling her close and kissing her lips until she dug a claw into him causing him to break the kiss.

"Damn you woman that hurt!"

"I meant it too as kissing you like that gives me thoughts that are best left for the night. And if you remember, that is what happened to you the first time your lips touched mine."

He laughed as he rubbed the spot where she had stuck him.

"Yes, I remember, and I was free of facial hair and you were flat chested."

She took his hand and with the other made a motion which unlocked the door to the chamber.

"Come, let us eat then get to work."

As they walked to hallway to the kitchen, she continued to brief Linus.

"I surveyed ever meter of this world and could not find a trace of mechanical advantage. No ruins or remains of a transport anywhere, but there is something beneath the palace according to sensor data, but I was never able to thoroughly examine the lower levels."

Linus stopped in his tracks causing Soraya to stop and turn to him.

"What are you thinking Linus?"

"A memory of long ago. From soon after I first came here. It's foggy but I seem to remember a door that was bricked up. I was a laborer carrying crude bricks from the hearth outside to where the brick layers were working."

He suddenly shuddered.

"Oh, all that's holy. When the job was finished, we were all put to the blade. Gia, I was murdered because I had seen that door. Murdered by the King's guard!"

She stepped to him and took him by the shoulders.

"Linus, control yourself. Let's eat and relax as you consider this further. I cannot fathom what you have experienced, but try to let the pain flow from your thoughts and hold onto the rest if you can."

Soraya was sadden by the way Linus/Cyril was reacting to his memories as she remembered him as being strong while also being considerate and gentle with others. The Council never spoke of why he was being punished, for what deed he had done to deserve his life up till now. It angered her that they had missed out of that time together but once this mission was complete, they had the rest of their lives to live as one.

They found the kitchen was lacking in many things as the siege had depleted much of its larder. She sent one of the kitchen help out to the checkpoint to find Steffen or Porsett and to have them return with them to the kitchen.

Soraya was eating a boiled potato and coarse bread when Steffen arrived. She told him to go to Roman, advise him the city is his and to bring food from the farms, so the people could now eat. It would do no good to continue to starve them as all it would accomplish was hatred against him and his people.

Linus had been quiet through the meal as he searched his memories of the palace in its early times. It had been added on many times over its existence and in a way, it was like a jig-saw puzzle of hallways, especially below ground.

They took a two liter jug of water with them as they began the search for the door he had helped close, starting on the level just below the main floor of the palace. The additions and different paint on the walls distorted his memory as they carefully walked every hallway on that level. Linus asked Soraya about the water since they could materialize what they needed without it. She told him it was for those eyes watching them as she was not ready to reveal who they were yet.

Down to the next level they walked, talking about his life without her as he served his sentence for the crime the Council held against him. As bad as Soraya wished to know what he had done to bring down the wrath of the Council on him, she never asked.

On this level they found a short hallway leading off another which had no doors, just a short hall going nowhere. This was puzzling to both of them. Soraya had Linus go back and guard the hall, so no one could interfere or witness with what she was going to do.

Soraya kneeled on the floor and closed her eyes as her body relaxed as she turned all her energy inward. Soon she stood leaving her body in place and walked to the end of the hall and through the wall then through a thick wooden door into a dark room.

A slight motion of her hands produced a bright blue plasma ball which just rested on the palm of her hand giving light to the room. It only took her a second to recognize this was an armory of modern weapons compared to what the people of this world had available to them. Rifles, pistols and other assorted weapons lined the walls and rested on tables within the room. She turned back to the door, stepped through it and the wall before snuffing out the plasma ball. She looked at her body thinking it had been decades since she had seen it was this vantage point then reentered it.

Soraya felt refreshed in taking that trip out of her body, but as her teacher had once warned her, staying out too long and too often can cause the spirit and flesh to begin to lose connections causing one to become less than the other.

She walked out of the small hall to Linus and put her arm around his waist.

"At the end of that hall is a wooden door and behind that door is an armory of modern weapons. Modern for the time the door was sealed and far superior to what is present on this world today."

"What next?"

"We go down another level and see what we can find there. As big as it was, that room was not large enough to produce the sensor readings I received in my survey ship."

"Alright, let's go."

"Are you feeling alright?"

He turned to her and shook his head.

"No, because if my memories are correct, I have children, adult children out in the population. Children I watched grow and start families before I died and was reborn."

"Cyril, Linus cannot make contact with them other then just smiling as you pass in the street. Their father and grandfather is dead and gone, leave him that way. Their life is theirs now and there is nothing you can do about it. Understand me?"

"Yes, I understand completely. Who gave you my pardon? The crystal which returned me to this life?"

"Mauricio gave it to me."

"He could have left out the memory spell, but I guess it is needed for me to know where I have been, and to recognize you as you are now older and even more lovely than I last saw you."

"Listen my love. The night you were bound by the Council was the night I was going to surrender myself to you. After all that time playing, being intimate and withholding myself, I was ready to let you take me as you did last night."

"And you waited all this time for me and did not take another?"

"That was evident after you took me last night and we had to clean ourselves afterwards. Many tried, both Delphian and human, but I had promised myself to you and I knew that the Council would eventually have to give you pardon so you could return to Delphi."

"You're an amazing woman Gia."

"I told you that before you gave me my first kiss, remember?" She laughed before she pulled his head down and kissed him.

They checked the next level with Cyril/Linus thinking the armory was the door he was involved with closing up.

On the lowest level they examined each hallway twice to insure they did not miss anything since anything buried beneath the palace had to be under this floor. As Linus turned to go up the stairs, Soraya had an idea.

Soraya went to the nearest door to the stairs and found it locked which did not slow her down as with a slight motion of the hand opened for her. She was glad she left her helm on the table in the dressing room as it would have recorded her movements and the conversations between her and Linus.

This room was also dark but when she snapped her fingers, torches long the walls ignited showing her it was about the size of the Queen's chambers, and bare of furniture or stored items. She walked the room looking at the walls, running her hand long them letting her fingers search for a concealed door but did not find one. She made the full circuit and was at the door where Linus was standing, watching her when her mind said she had seen something she had dismissed upon first glance.

Soraya turned back to the room and walked to the middle of it and looked up. In the ceiling was anchored a large eyelet. Looking down at her feet, the block of stone she was standing on her holes in it at the corners. She got down on her knees and brushed the dust away to see that the holes had bits of rust around them as if some type of metal once was embedded in the stone.

She walked back to Linus.

"What if the door we are looking for is actually a slab of stone in the floor?"

Linus closed the door and locked it before walking over to examine the floor. He stepped back and took a deep breath as he closed his eyes. Soraya watched as he was muttering to himself then she heard the grating sound of stone against stone as the one she had examined slowly rose from its position.

She moved closer and added her own strength to Linus's as the stone rose clear of the floor and she just held it above the floor as Linus moved it out of the way. Once clear she released her hold and Linus sat it down. She looked over at Linus and he was breathing hard and sweating.

"Are you alright Linus?"

"I should have transformed into Cyril but yes, I am alright. But I am certainly out of practice."

They both stepped to the hole to see blackness until Soraya ignited another plasma ball and dropped it into the hole. Guiding it down with her mind so it did not slam into the bottom extinguishing it.

"We found the anomaly Soraya. There is a ship down there."

Soraya clasped her bracelets together and transformed into Gia, then stepped into the hole and floated down as she ignited two more plasma balls. She set one on a ladder rung as she floated towards the bottom of the tunnel. When her feet touched the floor, she rolled the ball she had left down a corridor, then ignited another ball and rolled it down in the other direction.

She looked over at the tunnel entrance to see Linus's boots float down then she saw he had turned into Cyril for this adventure. Holding onto a transformation took a lot of power but in their natural state, they had complete control of that power in case danger lurked in this derelict buried beneath the palace.

Cyril/Linus could change normally, but Gia/Soraya had a spell placed upon her when she started her mission by the Council and it required her to use the bracelets to transform. Once they returned to Delphi, the spell would be removed, and she would not need the bracelets.

Slowly they moved through the ship, looking in very cabin, every space to find anything which might give them a clue to the name of the ship. The bridge was no help as it was stripped of anything which might indicate where the ship originated from builder. It was as if whoever buried it wanted all trace of ownership or shipyard removed from it. But one thing was quickly noticed was that this ship was not built for interstellar travel.

Based on the size of the ship, it would be fine for transport between planets in the same solar system, but beyond that it would be too slow for any value between systems. Its size also precluded commerce value outside of a system. But in the middle stage of interstellar exploration, ships such as this one were piggy-backed to interstellar transports and used as heavy duty shuttles where the primary vessel was not able to make planet fall and standard shuttles were too small for heavy equipment.

It was when they made it to the engine room that an indication of where the ship was built came to light. Wedged behind a cabinet was a manual for the environmental controls for the ship. Neither Cyril nor Gia recognized the model or type controls since they were not of their worlds, but it did remove the suspicion that Delphi was involved with seeding this planet. This would now require Soraya to contact the Searcher, and have the Fleet run a complete background on every ship built with this model controls, then locate or eliminate possible candidates from that list.

Now came the question of what happened to the mother ship that brought this one to this world? And why would someone strip all of the data plates off the ship?

Gia floated back up to the lower level of the palace first and by the time Cyril arrived she had already transformed back into Soraya. He looked at her and gave a heavy sigh as he transformed back to Linus.

"Why the heavy sigh?"

"From the first moment I laid eyes on you, I thought Gia was the most beautiful creature in the universe, but I have to say that Soraya is just as attractive, although I do like nibbling on your pointy ears."

She walked over to him, pulled his head down and kissed him as if she was going to take him right there. When she broke the kiss, she rubbed his crotch then laughed.

"Tonight, Linus can have Soraya and you decide whom you'd rather make love too, but no cheating."

Linus grinned then kissed her again.

They sealed the door to the room behind them as they started back up the stairs to the main floor.

"Soraya, what made you look in that room?"

"I just thought if I was going to hide an access to something I needed to haul supplies out of, why not put it at the stairs. And I just thought of something. The weapons. It might be possible to get a trace from serial numbers."

"Good thinking. Your time in the Fleet has served you well."

"It was interesting. Although I did miss our food. Have you any idea how hard it is to find a Fleet cook that can make a Lizard Pie?"

Linus laughed.

"I'd say that was impossible."

"You're right, it is."

Linus laughed again remembering the joke, the play they exchanged as children when she would make him a make believe Lizard Pie during their play dinner dates.

As they walked to the Queen's chambers, they discussed finding a different bedroom since they had no idea when the Queen would return. Linus said he knew of another room, with a nice, large bed that was being unused at the time of the King's demise.

When they entered the chambers, both heard Soraya's helm signaling a call alert. Soraya uncovered the helm and put it on.

"Soraya here, over."

"Soraya, this is Searcher, we have been trying to contact you for over an hour and a vid request to your AI only came back black, over."

"Yes Searcher, I left my helm in my temporary quarters while I went in search of the palace anomaly the sensors detected. Is there a problem, over?"

"Yes, Sector wants you off the planet immediately, over."

She paused for a moment before responding.

"Relay to Sector that I'm staying where I'm at for the time being. We found the anomaly and it is a ship buried beneath the palace. Send down the survey ship and I'll send up what we have found that needs investigation, over."

"Lieutenant Commander Khan, this is an order for you to leave the planet, over."

"Searcher, please advise Sector I refuse to leave at this time, over."

There was a long pause before a response to her refusal.

"Searcher will relay your reply. You said we a moment ago. Who is we, over?"

Soraya turned to look at Linus knowing the AI's vid would capture as he was standing there. She then pulled the helm off and using the internal switch, turned the power off to the helm.

"Was that wise Soraya?"

"Linus, I was given the option by the Council to expose us to the Federation. My first loyalty is to Delphi whether I'm Soraya or Gia. I was given the mission of bringing down the King, and I have done so, but now the Fleet or the Federation wants me gone before the mission is complete. These people are humans and need guidance as they move from a medieval society into one of democracy. To abandon them now would only bring chaos."

"Yes, you are correct. Right now, the people within the city fear you more than the former slaves but soon that will change, especially if any of the former slaves decide to seek revenge against their former masters."

"They call me witch, but all I have done is what any well trained female in the Fleet can accomplish. But if they do not wish to come together and build a world, I'll make them wish I was a witch."

"Gia, the Councils rules concerning interference with a fledging species. Have you forgotten them?"

"Cyril, we are not dealing with a fledging species here. What we are dealing with is a species in regression, or at least stagnant. But we know they did not arrive in that condition. We may never know what caused this situation, but there are people out there who have fought and killed to change their situation. Do we just turn our back on them now?"

She took a deep breath before continuing.

"I've killed dozens of men in the past months. Do I just live knowing I did such a thing then walked away before the final act of the play?"

"No. You're right, but what is the next step?"

"By my refusal to leave this world, the Fleet will be forced to send a ship of the line here to attempt to remove me. The Commodore may even come himself since he started me on this path. If so, these people will get a culture shock which I pray to the Gods will put them on the right path to rejoin humanity."

"This is a risky move on your part, but I shall stand with you as I do not wish to see any others harmed as I witnessed in the past lives I lived through."

Winging it

As Linus went to insure the scribes were producing as many copies of the Principles as possible, Soraya went to find Steffen to see why there had not been any food delivered to the palace. What she found was not to her liking.

"Soraya, I did as you instructed, but no one wants to give up even a morsel of bread to the city, and Roman will not speak with me." Steffen advised Soraya just outside of the camp.

She went into the camp to find Roman sitting in the shade of his shelter as if there was nothing in the world to concern himself with. From astride her horse, she spoke to Roman.

"Why are you not helping feed those in the city as they are on the verge of starving?"

"Since you have seemed to have taken over my quest, I just thought you could deal with things."

"Roman, you are acting like a spoiled child. Your quest is not complete until all of the people are united under a single banner, yet you are allowing for a further rupture between them."

"I do not know the meaning of your words, but they can rot as far as I am concerned."

"And what of Reita and the children she is carrying? She is one of them. Are you going to send her back to also starve because of your pettiness?"

"Again, I do not know your words."

Soraya became angry at Roman for his stubbornness and her own lack of handling the situation properly. She caused this situation by not keeping Roman informed, now she has to fix it. These people had lived their lives in fear, and in anger, she decided to show them real fear.

As she glared at Roman who was smugly smiling at her, she formed a plasma ball in her right hand. The trick with the plasma balls were the intensity in which they were formed. The blue ones were safe to handle and might scorch clothing if a person was hit with one, and a red one would certainly injure a person, while a gold one was like a grenade, capable of killing on contact. The one in her hand was gold.

Soraya brought her hand up so Roman could see the sparkling ball of plasma in her hand. His eyes got big as it looked as if she was holding a ball of fire. Her instincts got control of her emotions and she tuned the ball down to a pale blue ball then threw it at the gap between Roman's spread legs. It did explode on impact, sending dirt and pebbles onto him as he scrambled to get away.

"All that's holy!" He nearly screamed as he gained his footing.

As he came upright to look at her, she hit him in the chest with a heavier blue ball knocking him off his feet. Soraya swung her leg over the horses neck and dropped off onto the ground, then walked over to him as he was patting the smoldering material of his jerkin. She looked down at him, pointing a finger at him as she spoke.

"You have called me a witch many times, so be it, I will be what you wish I should be. You started a war Roman, and I finished it for you. Now you have to lead these people whether you wish to be a leader or not, because they look to you for guidance. All the people of this world are yours to care for now, so be a man and take care of those in need. Do it now before I become angry and forget my place on this world."

Soraya formed a gold plasma ball and threw it at a large tree as she turned back to her horse. The tree exploded and toppled to the ground. She looked back at Roman.

"Do not make me angry Roman."

She gathered the reins of her horse and walked it over to her shelter and the archers who viewed it all. Steffen had dismounted there as he waited for Soraya to confront Roman.

"Steffen, Anton, Porsett, all of you are free men to determine your own fate. I hold no bond against any of you and none of you owe me allegiance. But if this world is to move forward, prosper then the hatred for your once slave masters must cease. There are many former slaves, your brothers and sisters still in the city that are in need of food. Do what your conscious tells you to do from this time on."

She mounted her horse as Anton spoke up.

"Soraya, you are a witch who freed us from our slavery."

"Anton, I'm not a witch and in time you will learn that. Soon others will come, human just like you and they will bring all manner of things that seem like magic, but it is nothing more than knowledge and science, the very things you have been denied. Things I was born too and learned as a child."

"They have such knowledge in the mountains?" Steffen asked.

"No Steffen, I lied when I said I came from the mountains to make my path amongst you smoother. I come from far away. I come from the stars you see at night and it is from those stars your people first came, but that secret has been kept from you. Do not fear what is to come, but be ready for it."

She sat for a moment looking at the confused faces of the men before her.

"Steffen, you have been a good lieutenant. The Archers are yours now, lead them wisely. You have good lieutenants around you to help you smooth the way to final peace."

"Soraya are you leaving us?" Steffen asked.

"Not yet as there is much I still need to do. I came here to end a war and to find the one my heart belongs too. I have found that one that fulfills me, now the war must end, and it can only end when both sides join as one. Look deep inside each of you and you will find the peace each of you seek."

Soraya reined her horse away from the men and rode off back towards the city. Anton turned to Steffen and spoke.

"Steffen, witch or not, Soraya treated us as equals and gave us the knowledge to fight and defeat those who oppressed us. She always stood before us in the fight. Her words at night gave us wisdom even if we did not see it as that at the time. Soraya gave you lead and my bow and sword are yours to command. What shall we do now?"

Steffen looked at Soraya as she rode away.

"We finish this as she envisioned. Gather the archers. Gather the craftsmen. Then we gather the things the city needs to survive. We take everything and move to the city to provide and protect those that are not able to defend themselves as she often spoke of. Do it now."

As his men moved to saddle their horses, Steffen walked over to Roman who had stood watching Soraya talk to the archers.

"Roman, what Soraya spoke of is true. We must unite the people under one banner and it is yours that started this war. Help us or stay out of our way and do not interfere as we shall do as Soraya has asked of us. She asked, not ordered, and we shall do this for her as she freed us then gave us knowledge. What say you Roman?"

"My army greatly outnumbers your bows but if it came to a fight, you would kill too many of us before we could strike the first blow with a sword or lance. I did not understand all the words she used against me, but I did understand that this needs to be done and finished. We must do this together or all those who have died will be wasted. I place no bond on you Steffen, or your archers, but only ask that you stand with me in doing what Soraya says needs to be done here. Go do as she has told and if anyone denies you the things needed for the city, have them bring that argument to me. Soraya is right, it is time to finish this and to do so peacefully."

As Soraya rode towards the city she grasped the gold band on her wrist, drawing from its power to reach out with her mind.

"Father, if you can hear me, I am in over my head in this quest. I have found Cyril and we have bonded, but this world is torn asunder and I'm not sure I can find the glue to put it back together. I cannot leave this world as it is after the things I have done here. I shall continue to move towards the end, but it seems I am lost."

Just as she was about to give up in receiving a reply she felt a calm come over her then only one word came to her mind in the voice of her father: Soon.

Soraya was met at the palace steps by a guard who took her horse and told her he would care for it. She thanked him then took the steps two at a time as she had a thought as she rode through the city. It was the King's chambers she needed to investigate next.

When she entered the chambers, she sealed the door then went to the door that lead to the King's harem and sealed it. If there were still members of his harem in those rooms, she would see to them later but at the moment, this was more important.

As she was standing in the middle of the chambers, thinking of where a hidden door might be, she suddenly stiffened, trapped in her human body as it felt she was encased in a cage, unable to move. Her mind cried out as her body felt as if it was on fire then she collapsed on the cold, stone floor.

When she was finally able to move, the first thing she noticed was the pale blue of her hands as she braced herself to get up. She stood and walked over to a mirror to view herself. She was once again Gia, in full form as she wore the Soraya clothing. She closed her eyes and when she opened them, she was once again Soraya. She laughed as she understood what had happened. The

Council had returned all of her powers to her from the vastness of space. Soraya/Gia looked at her wrist bands and they just crumbled away, no longer needed.

Soraya turned away from the mirror and waved her hand across the room. All of the curtains, the furnishings vanished leaving only bare walls as if no one had ever lived in the room.

She laughed as she knew that her powers exceeded even Cyril's as she had over a thousand years of study and practice which he was denied during his time on this world.

It only took a moment before she found what she was searching for as the concealed door seemed to glow against the far wall. She walked to it and looked closely at the seam of the door then the floor beneath it. From the dust which sparkled she knew that this door had not been opened in decades, maybe hundreds of years. But it did not resist her as she ordered it open for her.

"Thank you, Father."

Soraya entered the hidden room to find a desk with an old computer sitting on it and books lying everywhere. She waved her hand and the decades of dust vanished from the surfaces as she moved to the desk. On the desk was a ships log book, bound in red leather with gold lettering on it. Soraya smiled and left things as they were as she left the room with the door closing and sealing it behind her.

With a wave of her hand, the chambers returned as they was, and she unsealed all the doors. Before exiting the chambers, she paused and sent out a sense of calm to the people of this world.

She made her way to the Queen's chambers and retrieved her helm. She no longer needed it to communicate with the Searcher, but it was still not time to open the Federation to whom she really was. Once she powered it up, she put it on and called the Searcher.

"Searcher, this is Soraya, over."

"Soraya, this is Searcher, go ahead over."

"Searcher request you do a search on the vessel Sequoia, over."

Soraya spelled out the name, so they would have it correctly.

"Understand Sequoia. Soraya be advised we have a response from Sector Fleet Headquarters concerning your refusal to return to the Searcher, over."

"Searcher let me guess. I am to consider myself under arrest, over."

"Affirmative Soraya, over."

"Advise Sector that the Commodore gave me this mission and I will only surrender myself directly to him. So, he had best get off his fat bottom and come here to get me. Searcher send that in my voice to Sector, over."

"Soraya be advised he is already on his way as we speak, over."

"Good. Now please find out all you can about the Sequoia as quickly as possible, over."

"Reason for search, over?"

"It appears it is the name of the ship that brought these people to this planet, over."

"Source of information, over?"

"I found a ships log book with that name on it, over."

"Thank you, Soraya, that will help to get Sector moving on the search for the ship's point of origin and last known transit. Where is the log book now, over."

"I left it where I found it along with other items including a computer, hidden in the palace. The room is sealed until the Fleet can take over here from me, over."

"Understand Soraya, over."

"Searcher, I'll contact you if and when I discover anything else. Soraya out."

She removed the helm and deactivated it again. She gathered up the rest of her things from the dressing room and left to find Linus which was not hard for her now as she could sense his location within the palace.

In the West tower, she found Linus in a musty room reviewing a parchment. She had to smile as the large room contained a crude, yet what appeared to be effective printing press. The operators of the press placed a sheet of parchment down then using a hand crank, pressed the parchment down on inked lettering, transferring the lettering to the parchment.

Linus looked up at her from his stool then handed her the parchment he was reading.

"How does this look to you?"

She quickly read the document then smiled.

"Yes, they have it as I dictated it. Very good."

Linus reached over and took her wrist, now bare of the bracelet. He never spoke but she knew the question in his mind.

"I am whole again."

Linus smiled then turned back to the scribes.

"Lady Soraya tells me you have done your work properly. Keep at it as we need many more copies to spread amongst the people."

He stood and took her hand, leading her out of the room and into the hallway.

"I sense you have found something."

Soraya told him of the hidden room in the King's chamber and what it contained from her casual examination of it, then she told of her conversation with the Searcher as they walked away from the printing room. He asked her how she was going to deal with the Fleet once the Commodore arrived.

"I shall deal with them as Gia. It is time the Federation knew they were not alone in this universe in their drive for peace. The Mordi along the East rim can be dealt with once the Federation knows we can communicate with them and stop the killing of both parties due to a gross misunderstanding. And with the Federations expansion in all directions, they will soon discover others that are even more dangerous than the Mordi"

"The Federation is at war with the Mordi? How'd this happen?"

She told him of the war that had been going on for nearly one hundred years as the Federation was expanding into Mordi space and the Mordi also slowly moving towards Federation space. With neither side able to communicate with the other, all they could seem to do was clash when they came together with great loss on both sides with the Mordi suffering the worst losses.

They talked as Linus guided them to a much smaller room with a bed large enough for both of them. Soraya placed the helm on a table and once again covered it since the Searcher could activate it remotely and she was not going to allow them to hear or see what happened in this room.

"Linus, whose room is this?"

"These are my quarters."

Soraya looked at the bed then motioned for the door to lock as her clothing fell away from her body.

"We have time on our hands now to do as we wish, and I wish to see if Linus is as good a lover as Cyril."

96

Linus just shook his head as his clothing also fell from his body. Soraya went to the bed and crawled upon it, motioning for him to join with her.

He took her twice over the afternoon before they were both exhausted and just lay entwined with each other.

"Well Soraya, are you pleased with me as Linus?"

"Very pleased but I think you cheated in a good way. But I must say I enjoyed the feel of your beard against me. I think Cyril would look nice with a beard such as Linus wears."

"So, it shall be. What are your plans now?"

"Rest, then wait for the Federation to make their appearance. Do you feel it?"

"Are you talking about the sense of relief within the city?"

"Yes, that."

"Yes. Your men must have obtained the food to feed the city."

"Yes, I was concerned that Roman would fight against that even after my talk with him."

"Talk with Roman? I do hope that whichever persona you are at that moment, the temper you had in your youth has mellowed because I remember you hurling a ball of fire at one of our classmates who angered you."

"He insists on calling me a witch, so I gave him a mild example of what this witch can do to get his attention. Do not worry, I only scorched him slightly."

"What am I to do with you my love?"

"Say the words that bond our spirits forever."

Linus released his hold on her and rolled out of bed. As she watched him, he was transforming into Cyril and once the transformation was complete, he had regal robes about him and the light beard she ask of him. He held his left hand out to her and she rose from the bed, transforming into Gia as she did so, with a silver gown sparkling with gems as she stepped off the bed onto the floor and took his hand in her left hand.

"Gia Soraya Khan, I, Cyril Maxam Dostler do ask that you accept my hand as my wife and bond mate."

"Cyril Maxam Dostler, I, Gia Soraya Khan accept your hand as you accept mine as my husband and bond mate."

"Gia Khan, do you forsake all others that may wish to have and hold you?"

"I do Cyril Dostler, do you also forsake those that wish to have you before me?"

"I do Gia. From this time forward we are bonded and married. Husband and wife."

"I accept your place as my husband and my place as your wife."

They took each other in their arms and kissed deeply as his robes and her gown vanished, leaving them in their Delphian form. Cyril took her back to bed and they consummated their wedding vows in that form. In a tradition which went back before mankind walked on the surface of the planet Earth, rings appeared on their left hands, but not rings of precious metal, but rings tattooed into the flesh, never to be removed and always a reminder of their bond.

When they rose later to eat, Gia just waved her hand which caused a table appeared covered with dishes of food and glasses of wine for them to feast upon. Cyril viewed the meal and told her that her cooking had improved since they were children. She flicked a fingertip fireball at him which he caught, then blew out as he laughed.

Exposure

Soraya and Linus spent the next three days mostly in his quarters with her working with Cyril on enhancing his powers from his time away from his studies when they were not moving around the palace and the city ensuring the people were taken care of.

Even in their human form, their rings were present, and Anton was the first to notice amongst her archers. Even though she had given Steffen command of the archers, they still looked to her for guidance. The King's army were also the city guards and came to recognize Linus's position as Soraya's mate, causing them to further accept her instructions. Soon the guards were accompanied by archers on the walls, and when Soraya sent a detail to bring those who had left the city back, the detail was led by an archer with members of the army included.

Three nights after they were officially bonded, Soraya transformed into Gia dressed as a young maiden which cause Linus/Cyril to laugh as he changed into a werewolf, and during the actual mating she also turned into a werewolf as she was being taken from behind. The next morning, they had to treat each other's claw marks from the mating, so they would not be seen by others.

Cyril told her never again as much fun as it was to play that game as children where actual mating did not occur, once the coupling took place, the passion and reactions to that passion was more than he wanted to experience twice. She agreed with him.

They were exploring the East tower of the palace looking for any additional items that might give them an indication of why this world turned out the way it did when Soraya laughed which caused Linus to ask why.

"Linus, the Fleet is entering orbit. Three vessels which includes a Marine Assault Carrier. Do they think they will need a Battalion of Marines to remove me from this world?"

He looked at her with a grin.

99

"Darling Soraya, I think they did not bring enough support even if all I did was sit back and watch. So, what are you going to do now?"

She closed her eyes for a moment then smiled as she opened them back up.

"I think I shall introduce them to Gia and get them in the proper frame of mind. I shall be back as soon as they understand this is not a situation where might will win the day."

Soraya transformed into Gia, gave Linus a kiss then vanished to reappear on the bridge of the Heavy Cruiser Bridgeport, the flag ship of Commodore Faria. The effect was immediate as the Marines who stood duty on the bridge began drawing their weapons to find themselves froze in space.

"Greeting Commodore Faria, welcome to Phaedra."

"Commander Khan?"

"Yes Commodore, there is much to tell you, but the bridge is not the place. I shall meet with you again in one hour in the conference room. This world needs attention that normal diplomatic methods which will not be fruitful. In one hour, Commodore."

She vanished form the bridge and the Marines were released from their condition looking for the invader that had appeared before them. She returned to the tower laughing still in the form of Gia.

"Alright my love, why the laughter?"

"The looks on everyone's faces when I popped in on the bridge, and those poor Marines I had to freeze in place as they were drawing their sidearms to defend the bridge. Poor things."

"Gia, that's not nice, laughing at them as they were doing what they were supposed to do."

She stopped laughing.

"I'm sorry Linus, you are right, but if you had seen some of the expressions, you probably would have laughed too."

"Anyway, you were not gone long."

"I told them I would meet with them in an hour in the ship's conference room. This way we'll not be interfering with bridge operations."

"We? Are you expecting me to attend this meeting?"

"As Linus you know this world better than I do. As Cyril you can also reinforce my warnings about venturing too deep into space without using extreme caution."

"Yes, I'm surprised they have not made contact with the Tranters yet."

"In a way they have. The Tranters established a colony closer to the Eastern rim of Federation space and for several hundred years kidnapped humans, captured numerous ships, for their breeding colony. The Council arranged for one ship to be taken which carried a disease which wiped out the entire colony. Sadly, many humans were released from their breeding pens and were turned loose into the wilderness to survive on their own. That world is now quarantined by the Federation since the surviving humans have turned cannibal. But at the rate of expansion by the Federation, within a decade, if not sooner, they will encounter the Tranters in their home space."

"They are vicious little beasts. So how do you want to do this?"

They spent the rest of the time preparing for the meeting. Linus would make his appearance before becoming Cyril later in the meeting. He was to also watch those in the conference room since Gia would most likely be distracted by questions from the Commodore and whoever else may be in the room.

Gia changed back into Soraya as they went back to his quarters to collect her helm and the manual since the Searcher did not send down the survey craft to collect those things. She was not going to change into Gia until in the conference room so those present would witness the change. Since she knew where they were going to transport too, she took his hand and in a blink of an eye they were standing in the conference room causing everyone in the room to almost jump back away from them.

Soraya looked around the room to see people standing behind them and she motioned them to move to the other end of the room before speaking.

"Commodore Faria, Ladies and Gentlemen, for those who do not know me, I am Lieutenant Commander Soraya Khan, survey officer for the planet Phaedra, or OB-5547 as listed in the Federation catalog."

She changed into Gia, keeping Soraya's apparel for the time being.

"This is my true appearance. I am the High Priestess Gia Soraya Khan of Delphi, and I am at your service. This gentleman beside me is King's Lieutenant Linus Dostler of the Palace Guard who is known to me, and trusted by me. Linus show them Cyril."

Linus changed into Cyril in regal robes.

"I am Grand Master Cyril Maxam Dostler, of Delphi. For a thousand of your years I was exiled, banished from my home to serve my banishment on Phaedra as punishment for a crime against the laws of the Delphian people. I lived and died many times to be reborn as a slave or a freed man during that time without memory of each life until my exile was pardoned and the memory of who I really am was restored. I am at your service."

There was both a look of amazement and terror spread about the room as they spoke. Gia put forth a sense of calm and in seconds the terror that many felt melted away.

"Commodore, we will answer any and all questions with as much honesty as possible with the exception of where Delphi is located in the universe."

The Commodore straightened up in his chair and cleared his throat.

"What do I call you?"

"Sir, I will answer to either Gia or Soraya. Which ever is easier for you."

"I don't know where to begin under these conditions."

"Commodore begin as if it was just Lieutenant Commander Khan standing before you."

"Yes, that would be easier. Commander, why did you refuse to return to the Searcher once you knew it was an order from Sector?"

"Because the world below us was at the threshold of destruction. For me to just disappear would have had the effect of unleashing the strong against the weak as former slaves would have seeked vengeance against their former masters. They thought I was a witch as I did things, simple things which I taught others, but I did have to give them a final display for them to understand their place in things."

Gia extended her hand and a light blue plasma ball formed in it. She stepped to the conference table and set it on the table, then rolled it to the Commodore.

"Catch it Commodore but be careful, if you squeeze it too hard it will burst and could injure your hands."

He caught the ball and then laughed.

"It is cold to the touch, yet it looks like fire inside."

"Yes, but this one can blow a hole through thirty centimeters of armor."

103

She produced a gold plasma ball and just rolled it around in her hands before tossing it in the air for Cyril to catch.

"It's all in understanding what you wish to do."

"Are you shapeshifters?" A question from an unknown civilian female.

"Who are you Madam?" Cyril asked.

"I am Marta Gonzales. I am a Xeno-biologist."

"We are not shapeshifters in the true sense. We have the ability to change our appearance as needed for indefinite periods of time, and although our normal appearance is different from yours, we are still human in context." Cyril responded.

"Pardon, my observation, but your appearance is that of Elves from Old Earth lore."

Cyril smiled.

"Of course, we do, since it is our visitation to your Earth that gave the Earth people that lore."

He suddenly changed into a depiction of an Earth Elf in earth tone clothing, and the light pink skin. He stood like that for a moment before changing back.

Gonzales laughed before commenting again.

"So, the lore of shapeshifters is from your people also?"

It was Gia who responded.

"No, they do exist, but unlike when we shift, we can also change our apparel to match our situation, they can only change their form, leaving their clothing as it was. If you wish to view it from this position, their change is physical, biological, where ours is magical."

"So, you're are a witch and he is a warlock?" Asked one of the ship's officers.

"No Commander, I am a Sorceress as Cyril is a Sorcerer. Witches are vulgar creatures who like to play with their food."

Cyril laughed at her joke knowing the truth behind it.

The question and answer period lasted for nearly a half hour before the Commodore put a stop to it.

"Alright Gia, now could you please explain to me what is happening here today?"

"Commodore, you broke the rules sending me down to Phaedra, and once again you must break the rules. But this time I will smooth the way for you and if need be, stand before Parliament to explain our actions. Hopefully by now you have information on the vessel Sequoia which we found buried beneath the palace. When I return to the surface, I intend to introduce the leaders of Phaedra to that information and show them the ship that brought their ancestors to this world."

Gia waved her hand and a delicate tea set appeared at their end of the table. She poured a cup and handed it to Cyril then one for herself and took a sip before continuing.

"With the Fleets expansion into unknown regions of space, you will soon encounter other creatures, some docile, some aggressive. You are currently in a war with the Mordi which we can mediate for the Federation and bring that war to an end."

"Mordi? Are you referring to the aliens along the East rim?" The Commodore inquired.

Gia made a simple movement with her left hand as she sipped on her tea. In the center of the table the form of a Mordi appeared, slowly rotating to give everyone a complete view of the creature. Once it had made two full rotations, she whisked it away.

"Yes, my people have had contact with them long before humans left Earth. We can converse with them and hopefully find peace between your two races. But soon you will encounter the Tranters. There is no negotiating with them. They are a violent race and consider themselves superior to all others, even my own, yet we have taught them to avoid us. You have already witnessed what they are capable of on the quarantined planet Prince Michael discovered."

She made another motion with her hand and a full grown Tranter appeared on the table showing its double rows of needle teeth. As before she removed it after two rotations.

"Those aliens are known as the Tranters?"

"Yes. It is important that the people of Phaedra are taken into the Federation before the Tranters reach out for a new food source as they would wipe the world clean of human and animal life for their larders."

"How do you suppose we do that without violating Alien Species Act?"

As Gia laughed, Cyril loudly clapped his hands. He didn't need to do this, but it was more for show than requirement. Suddenly everyone within the conference room found themselves in the King's chambers still sitting at the table or standing in the same positions they had as the moment he clapped his hands.

Both Gia and Cyril were back as Soraya and Linus as they appeared in the bed chambers. Soraya snapped her fingers and the large bed vanished giving them more room then she clapped her hands and a new group appeared in the room.

This group consisted of Roman and Queen Reita, along with Roman's chief Lieutenant's and Eli. Also, here were Steffen, Anton, Hammel, and the rest of her personal group of archers along with Trent.

All of the Rebels were reaching for their swords or knives when they realized they were unarmed.

"Be still all, you have nothing to fear today." Soraya spoke then she snapped her fingers again and a comfortable chair appeared.

"Queen Reita, a chair for you in your condition. Please sit as I make the introductions."

"Roman, remember my telling you that there would be those who would come to assist you. Let me introduce them to you."

"Commodore Faria please stand."

Faria stood.

"Commodore is a rank, a position within what is known as the Federation Fleet. If you will notice his dark fur, such as an animal might wear but he is no animal, he is as human as you are or the rest of the men with you. His race are known as Centaurians and Roman, if one hundred Centaurians had faced your army at the river, they would have killed all of you without pause as they are fierce warriors in battle."

She paused.

"Doctor Mullins please stand."

Mullins stood.

"Doctor Mullins is an Altairian physician. Her lovely skin color comes from her world and marks her race. The Altairians are people who are dedicated to healing and science. There is no magic in what they do, but hard work and study. Thank you, Doctor."

"The Federation is made of many races who have joined together to secure peace out amongst the stars. They are bound by oath to cause no harm and can bring knowledge that has been denied you for the existence of your ancestors arriving on this world."

She changed into Gia while leaving her clothing as Soraya.

"Roman you called me a witch, but I have powers far above what a witch could hope for. I am a Delphian and we are sworn to protect developing races of humans and non-humans from the dangers of the universe. I was sent here to find the man you know as Linus and to end the conflict on this world."

Linus stood for a moment before changing into Cyril, then he spoke to the Rebels.

"I am also known as Cyril and I too am a Delphian. I was exiled to this world soon after your ancestors arrived and have lived over a hundred lives as I unknowing waited for Gia to rescue me. Gia and I are now mate bonded."

Roman spoke up.

"Soraya is this the man you told me you were looking for?"

"Yes Roman, I knew he was on this world but did not know how he would look to me after all of these years we have been apart because of his exile."

She stepped over to Cyril and took his hand, then indicated the hidden door which became uncovered and opened.

"Commodore, in that room you will find the log book of the Sequoia and other files which may give you information concerning how these people came to this world. In case no one noticed, we have given each of you the ability to understand the speech of the others so there can be no misunderstanding during conversation."

"Gia, what are you and Cyril going to do now that you have joined us with the natives?" It was the Commodore who asked the question.

"Commodore, Cyril and I have a thousand years to make up for, but we shall be near if needed. Do not look for us but call our names and we shall hear and respond. When the time comes we will show all of you the ship that is buried beneath the palace, until then, take this time to learn of one another."

As they vanished, chairs for all standing appeared in the room. No one knew where to start until Eli moved a chair to the table and sit down and looked at the Fleet officers.

"I am Eli. Tell me about this Fleet and Federation Soraya spoke of."

In Linus's quarters, two lovers were engaged in the act of consummating their love for one another.

Passages

Gia was called back to the meeting as there was a question on how Roman's people could contact the Bridgeport when needed. She suggested bringing the Searcher down outside the city and introduce the people to the crew. Gia mentioned that the sooner the population is exposed to what exists in space, the sooner they could get used to the idea they are not alone in the universe.

She also mentioned to Reita that there should be recommendations on whom from the city that should take part in future meetings. It would take three more meetings before Gia felt the people of Phaedra were properly represented in the meetings.

The Searcher sitting outside the gates caused problems of a type no one anticipated. Once the initial shock of the space craft being on the ground was past, people were nearly crawling all over it in amazement. Gia suggested a section of Marines to control those coming near the Searcher and the Commodore agreed.

It only took two days before one of Roman's men made unwanted advances to one of the female Marines guarding the Searcher. She handed off her carbine to another Marine and then placed the man in a very uncomfortable position much to the amusement of his friends that were with him.

The Marines further made their capabilities known by setting up apples on stakes at fifty paces and easily shooting them off the stakes first with their carbines then with their pistols. When the word was spread amongst the population, the Searcher became less of an attraction.

Doctor Mullins pulled the Marines Corpsmen from their carrier and set up two clinics, one in the city and the other in the Rebel encampment. Roman was the first to attend the clinic at Gia's suggestion, so the Rebels would know it was safe to attend to have their illnesses or injuries taken care of. One thing the females of the planet accepted with ease were the implants to prevent pregnancy.

Gia and Cyril maintained their Delphian appearance as they moved about the city and the palace, even when they went to the Rebel encampment to check on progress. As foods slowly became scarce, Gia advised Roman to send the former farm slaves back to the farms to grow and harvest the crops growing there to feed the world's population. Within a month, the Rebel encampment was nearly empty except for those who had once worked in the quarry who stayed near the city.

It was during this time that Gia opened the concealed armory and had the Marines empty the room of all weapons and equipment, shuttling it up to their Assault Carrier and each item inspected for serviceability. The weapons themselves were in decent shape even after being stored for such a long time without maintenance checks done on them, but it was felt that the ammunition was not safe to utilize due to deterioration of the materials composing the sample lot.

When Commodore Faria was ordered to return to Sector Headquarters to answer why he had violated the Alien Species Act, Gia advised him to stay in place as per a minor paragraph in the Act where the senior officer on the scene could be required to remain on the scene upon the request of the representatives of a newly discovered Alien Species, and since she fell into the category, she made the request in video form, and it was sent to Fleet Headquarters in reply to the orders.

The video of her in shimmering silver gowns as it seemed butterflies circled her head turned the Federation Parliament upside down wondering what manner of trickery was being played upon them. Gia had set the stage for a delegation from Parliament to come to Phaedra to investigate this unique individual or was the video doctored to show what they had seen?

As time drew near for Reita and the maids to give birth to Roman's children, he brought them back into the palace, into the Queen's quarters and the quarters the maids once lived in with the living conditions improved with the help of Marine Engineers with the approval of the Commodore.

Doctor Mullins established a clinic inside the palace for all to use but with the knowledge that with the Queen carrying twins and five maids, there would soon be seven infants needing delivered and care. They had not consider seven other females who came to the clinic when they started their labor.

As Reita was delivering the twins by natural child birth, the rainy season began. This turned the roads into mud making it difficult for wagons to travel from the farms to the city to bring food. The Commodore authorized shuttles to transport food and both Marine and Fleet Engineers with the help of the former quarry workers, began harvesting crushed stone to lay on the roads to make them passable. The engineers taught the former slaves how to operate and maintain the equipment which harvested the stone at a rate the former slaves never dreamed of with less risk of harm.

The engineers also taught men plumbing as they improved the sanitation at the quarry, at the farms and especially in the city. Portable fusion generators and pumps were brought down from the ships in orbit to prove a better supply of water to the city first, then out to the different areas needing it.

With the disruption of lives as slaves became citizens, select former soldiers, along with some former slaves learned the principles of law enforcement and hand-to-hand fighting from the Marines, and were made Marshall's to keep the peace within the city. All of these individuals were examined by the Fleet's Psych Doctors to insure they were as unbiased as possible. This became necessary as there was still animosity between the former slaves, and those that once benefited from their labors.

Some Marines and Fleet personal taught crafts they had learned from their parents as children to those that desired to learn and in doing so established some cottage industries. Until the new Phaedra governing council could get organized, the system of barter was in effect. Services for services, goods for services, services for goods, and goods for goods.

Gia and Cyril became a common sight walking around the city in clothing similar to that worn by the common citizen and only donned their elegant robes when called for. Several female children were born and named Gia after her and some even named Soraya. Cyril also was honored in such a manner.

As they day came close for the arrival of the delegation from Parliament, the Fleet personnel worked even harder at improving the situation of the people of Phaedra because they were unsure what their civilian leaders would do once they arrived on a Heavy Cruiser which also contained the Fleet Admiral.

An Unexpected Guest

Two weeks before the delegation from Parliament was to arrive, a ship entered orbit that was completely unexpected. This ship was a single purpose warship detailed for the transportation of the Duke of Denoyelles family, the Royal family of the Federation.

On board the Heavy Cruiser Intrepid was the Duchess Karlie Gannaway, who was now in her sixties and had traveled to Phaedra to see if any of her charities could be of service to the people of Phaedra. With the transit time from the Royal Palace on Keres less that the Federation Capital on Hanover, her journey was much quicker than the delegations.

It was well known within the Federation that the Duchess had no problem getting down and dirty in both politics and helping others as she would help dig a garden, or build a new home after a natural disaster if another hand was needed. When she married the Duke, she was a Lancer Fighter pilot and before that a Lancer Scout. Her callsign as a pilot was Blade from her known usage of a knife as a Scout.

When she stepped off her shuttle, she was dressed in a simple jumper as if she was ready to go to work, instead of inspecting the possibility of needs for the community. The only thing that separated her from her entourage was her age, and the fact she was accompanied by Lancer Female Centaurians who acted as her personal body guards.

She was greeted by the Commodore, Gia and Cyril, along with Roman acting as representative of the former slaves, and a gentleman named Morrice, who represented the city. Eli was present as he had been appointed as President of the Council after several days of debate with Roman fighting against being President due to his lack of education.

The Duchess extended her hand to the Commodore as she approached the group.

"Commodore Faria, it is a pleasure to finally meet you."

He took her hand and bowed his head before speaking.

"Your Highness, it is an honor."

"Stow that Your Highness nonsense Commodore. I'm here to find out what needs to be done to help these people before the chair warmers from Parliament arrives."

The Commodore chuckled.

"Still a Lancer, are we?"

She grinned.

"You'll have to ask the Duke that, but even at our age, he has no complaints."

This caused the Commodore to give a loud belly laugh as the Duchess stepped to Gia, who curtsied.

"Lady Gia, your picture does not do your beauty justice."

"Duchess, I thank you and I can see how you attracted the Duke."

"Gia, we can stand here for hours complementing each other but what do you say you call me Karlie and I'll just call you Gia."

"Duchess, I am still listed as a serving officer in the Fleet."

"No, if my briefing packet is correct, Soraya Khan is listed as serving, not Gia Khan."

Gia laughed as she nodded her head.

"You are correct Karlie. May I introduce my husband, Cyril Dostler?"

Gia then introduced Karlie to the others present, then Karlie introduced her four bodyguards as attendants with only the Phaedrans not aware of their true purpose. As Karlie was doing this, Gia and Cyril changed clothing from royal robes to more functional clothing to match how the Duchess was dressed. Karlie noticed this out of the corner of her eye and turned to Gia.

"Gia, I wish you could teach me that trick. You have no idea how many times during a formal dinner I find my gowns are not very comfortable, yet I cannot break away to go change."

Gia chuckled.

"Karlie, this was one of the first things we learned as children. Our mothers taught this to us, so we could change our own diapers."

Karlie broke out in laughter as did her attendants and the Commodore. The others looked puzzled until Karlie explained what a diaper was, which then brought chuckles from them. She then turned to Eli and spoke to him.

"President Eli, please show me the city and maybe we can discover what my charities can do to help your situation."

They spent the day walking through the city, with Karlie speaking to many she met in passage, getting a feel for the city and it's inhabitants. Karlie was amazed at the way Gia and Cyril was treated as if they were normal humans even though they were in their Delphian form.

When they were offered a meat on a thin stick at a small stall within the city, one of the female Centaurians named Dita started to check it with a Pocket Doc to insure it was safe for the Duchess to eat, but Gia stopped her before it became obvious what she doing.

"Dita, there is no need to embarrass or insult our host. The food is safe to eat."

"Lady Gia how certain are you of this?"

"Do you think as a serving Fleet officer I would allow any harm to come to the Duchess?"

With a slight movement of her hand, Gia produced a small Chickleberry pie and handed it to Dita. Chickleberry pies were considered a delicacy to Centaurians. Dita laughed as she accepted the pie. Dita started to cut the pie to share with her sister Centaurians when Gia produced three more, one for each one of Karlie's guards.

The Centaurians ate the pies as Karlie nibbled on the meat telling their host how flavorful it was, and thanked him for it a second time before moving on. Cyril produced damp cloths for the Centaurians to clean their mouths and fingers with after finishing the small pies.

That evening Gia hosted a dinner in the King's former bed chambers which had been converted into the Council Meeting room. It was a buffet style dinner and as they ate, the Duchess posed a question to both Gia and Cyril.

"Gia, Cyril, if I am imposing, forgive me, but how do you produce things out of thin air?"

Gia nodded to Cyril to answer the question.

"Karlie look around you. Subtract all that is obvious and what do you see?"

"Cyril, if I understand you correctly, I see nothing."

"Correct in some ways but wrong in many others. Now relax and do not be frightened at what is about to happen."

Cyril never made a motion but Karlie suddenly gasped.

"Now Karlie, what do you see?"

"Its as if I am underwater, surrounded by all manner of things floating around me."

Suddenly she was back to normal.

"Karlie, the essences of life itself floats around us, the trick is recognizing it, and knowing how to assemble those particles into

117

something with substance. Even in the void of space, those particles, atoms if you wish are all around us. We Delphians are both blessed and cursed with the ability to assemble them with just a thought. We also draw our power from those same atoms."

Karlie sat for a long time moving her goblet around the table before speaking again.

"Are you capable of reading another person's thoughts?"

"Yes." Gia answered. "But we are forbidden from doing so with the exception of our bonded mates, and even then, it is wise to avoid such a thing. This skill develops later in our upbringing and before we have that ability, we are trained in how to deal with it. If we cannot put that ability aside, then we would be overwhelmed with the thoughts of those around us. Sadly, some are never able to construct that block and are driven insane by it."

"And before you ask, yes, we could use that power to influence others, which is an even more serious crime. Even this far from Delphi, the Council would know of our use of such power." Cyril injected into the conversation.

"Are you Gods?" Marleen, one of the Centaurians asked.

"No Marleen, we are not Gods, we are just different from humans." Gia answered. "Now Karlie, I have a question of you."

"Certainly Gia, ask it." Karlie replied.

"Are you here to insure the Commodore is safe from review by the Parliaments inquiry?"

Karlie smiled as she looked at the Commodore.

"No. In fact, the Duke has notified the people enroute to review this situation that my sole purpose here is for my charities, and that they are not to take my presence as being in support of the Commodore. While the Duke and I both agree that the restrictions of the Alien Species Act can be too restrictive, it is still up to the

Parliament to make any adjustments to it, not the Throne since it was Count Conrad who specified the act."

Karlie took a drink of wine before continuing.

"Gia, you used Soraya's knowledge as a survey officer of the Alien Species Act when you requested the Commodore's assistance her on Phaedra. Be prepared for some of those coming here to say you had no authority to do so since your alter-ego is that of a serving officer, and you are not of this world. The Throne will not interfere with the Alien Species Act, even at the cost of a dedicated Fleet Officer as the Commodore."

"Duchess, I could have denied Gia's request, but my conscious could not turn away from the needs of the people here on Phaedra." The Commodore spoke up.

"Yes Commodore, you responded to a humanitarian crisis, which is well within your powers as Sector Commander, and since these are humans who seem to have been placed here by a fail expedition, they could be described as apart from the Alien Species Act. Now we have other things to discuss before I return to the Intrepid."

During the tour of the city, it was noticed hundreds of school aged children moving around without meaning when they could be in school. Karlie surprised everyone when she told those present that on board the Intrepid were ten qualified teachers who had volunteered to come to Phaedra to set up a school based upon the reports from Soraya of the lack of education on the planet.

It the cargo hold of the Intrepid, were crates of books written in Spanglish since it was the language of the planet. They just had to find a location for a school, then gather the children up and start the process of educating them.

Included in the crates were paper and writing instruments so the children would not have to utilize the charcoal pencils and parchment that was used to write with as they learned about the universe.

119

Investigation

Commodore Faria was in the Searcher using their Comm to talk to the delegation aboard the Cruiser Avenger when it entered orbit around Phaedra. The Chairman of the delegation insisted that he come to the Avenger to face the delegation concerning the possible violation of the Alien Species Act.

When he asked the Chairman, who was from the planet Stratton, to come down a look at the work that had been accomplished, the chairman had a belligerent tone to his voice as he refused to shuttle down to see the work the Fleet had accomplished in the time they had been there.

Gia was standing off to the side, out of view of the vid camera and was developing a dislike for this Minister of Parliament. She looked at Cyril and grinned which caused him to smile and nod his head. She just took a breath then they were standing in the Palace Meeting room with the Commodore and the Delegation as the Chairman was in mid-sentence, dressing the Commodore down for his insistence they come down to the planet.

The Commodore turned, looking for Gia.

"Gia, what have you done?"

"Commodore, I did what I wished."

"Who are you?" The Chairman was nearly screaming as he pointed at Gia.

"Minister Cheever, I'm the person who requested that the Commodore make a presence here on Phaedra. Did you think I was an artificial image? A computer construct?"

"You can't be real!"

Gia removed her clothing to present her nude body to the Minister and the delegation standing behind him.

"Oh, I am very real as you can see, and my husband can attest too."

Her clothing returned to her body as she stepped closer to the Commodore, to stand beside him.

"Now tell me Minister Cheever, why is it you did not wish to come down to Phaedra?" Her tone was soft, almost musical as she spoke.

Cheever did not reply to her question, only stood shaking as he looked at her. Gia then spoke to the Commodore.

"Commodore notice anything odd about your inquisitors?"

The Commodore looked the men over twice then it dawned on him what Gia was talking about.

"The Admiral of the Fleet is missing. Did you exclude him?"

"No Commodore, I did not, but I believe the Delegation Chairman has. Minister Cheever, where is Admiral Manafort?"

"I…. I don't have to answer you, witch!" Was his reply.

Gia laughed and once more the sound of her voice was musical as she held up her index finger of her right hand as a blue flame erupted from it.

"Gia, use caution here." Cyril commented.

"Oh, my husband, I plan on using caution. I shall only give him a light burn, maybe take his eyebrows off."

Cheever's eyes grew large as he looked at the fire from her finger. As he spoke, Cheever's words sounded more like a plea, than a response.

"He's in his quarters! The Admiral is in his quarters!"

"No, he isn't Minister." She turned slightly to her right. "Admiral Manafort, welcome to Phaedra."

Admiral Manafort, the head of the Federation Fleet was standing to the side, away from the others with papers in his hand.

"Well, that was different." He spoke up as he looked at Gia. "You must be the one called Gia, or is it Lieutenant Commander Soraya Khan?"

"Admiral I shall respond to either name, although I am adorned as Gia at this time. Sir, can you tell us why you were not in the conference room with the delegation when they contacted the Commodore?"

The Admiral smiled as he looked at Gia then at the delegation as they had drawn closer to gather, almost cowering before her.

"I have been excluded from all hearings by Minister Cheever with approval of the President Swenson in this matter."

"Then why are you here if you have no part in this investigation?" Cyril asked.

"It seems I am here to place Commodore Faria under arrest for violation of the Alien Species Act and Mutiny once the investigation is complete." He replied to Cyril's question.

Gia looked at Cheever as her entire hand erupted in fire.

"Is this true Minister Cheever?"

Cheever fainted.

Gia just shook her head then addressed the other Ministers.

"Would one of you care to answer my question concerning the Admiral?"

No one spoke in response to Gia's question. She sighed and shook her head as the Duchess and her Centaurians appeared in the room.

"Damn Gia, give a person some warning will you!" The Duchess exclaimed as she seemed to slightly stagger forward, getting her footing under control. She looked around the room then turned to Gia.

"Gia, I thought we discussed this before the delegation arrived that I am not to have any part in this."

"Your Highness, we did and at the time I agreed with your position, but there seems to be a plot afoot which the Duke may not be aware of concerning Commodore Faria."

"Really now. Explain that, then explain why a Minister of Parliament is laid out on the floor."

Gia explained what had been said prior to Karlie being brought into the room. Then why Cheever was laid out on the floor. Admiral Manafort confirmed what Gia had said including that Cheever had only fainted. The Duchess just stood looking at Cheever on the floor before speaking.

"Dita, see to the Minister." Karlie instructed as Dita was the medical specialist of her guards. She then turned her attention to the remaining Ministers.

"Gentlemen would one of you care to explain why the Admiral was being excluded from the hearings with Commodore Faria?"

One young Ministers slightly stepped forward.

"Your Highness, Cheever told us that there was a plot within the Fleet to undermine the Alien Species Act and that Admiral Manafort could not be trusted to judge Commodore Faria during the hearings."

Karlie looked at the Minister then shook her head before turning to her guards.

"Nakato, my cube please."

Nakato opened her shoulder bag and removed a plain, wooden cube and handed it to Karlie who then walked over to the conference table and sat it down. She pulled the top part of the wood covering off to reveal a sparkling crystal cube and touched the side of the crystal with her finger. Less than a minute later a form appeared above the crystal. The form of her husband, the Duke Denoyelles.

"Yes Karlie?"

Karlie laid out all she knew up to that moment and had Admiral Manafort give what he knew before Karlie had the delegation move to the crystal and explain their side of the story. Dita had revived Cheever by this time and had him sitting in a chair away from the conference table. The only persons who did not speak to the Duke in this manner was Ghia and Cyril.

"Commodore Faria, have you seen the report on the vessel Sequoia?" The Duke asked.

"No Sire, I have not."

The Duke nodded before speaking again.

"Admiral Manafort, I think you need to take a hard look at your Intelligence section when you return to Denoyelles as the Commodore should have received a copy of the report by now."

"Sire, I have a copy of the report but sadly I do not understand your reference to it."

"Admiral if you have the report, then you know that the vessel Sequoia was part of an exploration out of Ishtar to find and open new worlds for exploiting the natural resources of that world. This was prior to Count Conrad ascending the Throne by several hundred years and the implementation of the Alien Species Act. By an odd coincidence, President Swenson's ancestors are from Ishtar."

No one spoke as it seemed the Duke was collecting his thoughts. When he next spoke, it was to Gia who was out of his view.

"Lieutenant Commander Khan."

Gia stepped into view of the crystal.

"Yes, Sire."

He looked at her for a moment before speaking.

"The Duchess was correct, you are very lovely in your natural form. Now the Duchess has informed me that your race has the ability to read minds. Did you use that ability to force this situation there on Phaedra today?"

"No Sire, that is a serious violation of my peoples laws. But I did sense something was out of place and I wanted answers. Sire, I placed the Commodore in the situation he is currently in, and I accept full responsibility in this matter."

"Lieutenant Commander Soraya Khan. I expect your resignation from the Fleet to be in the hands of Admiral Manafort by the end of the day on Phaedra. I do not expect it as a manner of punishment for your actions concerning Phaedra, nor your deception in entering first the Fleet Marines, then the Fleet. I expect it so any conflict between your oath as Soraya Khan and your true position as Gia Khan is removed from the equation. Is that understood?"

"It is clearly understood Sire, and it shall be done."

"Good, see to it. Admiral Manafort, as you know I work hard to stay out of the daily business of the Fleet and the investigation into Commodore Faria's conduct concerning Phaedra is included in that. Having said that, I instruct you to take charge of the investigation and you will make the final decision on Commodore Faria's status within the Fleet without interference by the Parliament or the Throne. This situation is both a political and a command problem, but as we both know, the commander on the scene must often set aside the rules and go with what is best at that moment in time. See to your duty Admiral."

"It shall be done Sire."

The Duke never responded beyond that point as he disconnected the communications from his end.

When Admiral Manafort turned to Gia, she was holding a document out to him which he took. It was her formal resignation from the Fleet giving her reason for dismissal as Unlawful Entry into Service. He tore it up and smiled.

"Find a better reason because I am not accepting that one as it would look badly against such an outstanding service record."

She handed him a second document which seemed to appear out of thin air. He read it and nodded, then handed it to the Commodore.

"Yes, I accept that one and will forward it to Headquarters when I return to the Avenger. Now Ministers, shall we all be seated at this table and get down to business?"

As the Ministers moved to the table the Admiral once again spoke to Gia.

"Miss Khan, would it be too much to ask that my aide and Yeoman are present to record this meeting?"

Gia flipped her hair with her left hand and the Admiral's aide and Yeoman were standing beside her.

"Not a problem Admiral."

The Admiral laughed then took his seat.

"Miss Khan, scientists have been working on teleportation for eons, yet your people do it so well and easily."

"Admiral, its not as easy as it seems." Cyril commented. "Somewhere out in the universe there is a stuff animal I lost when learning how to teleport. It was my favorite bedtime animal too."

Gia starting laughing and it became infectious around the table as it seemed to break the tension. Karlie had collected her cube and bid farewell since she had other things to do and left before the hearings started. Minister Cheever just sat, defeated, even though he had lightly chuckled at Cyril's comments.

The hearing lasted for over an hour with Gia assisting in retrieving the Commodore's personal log from his cabin along with his aide who had been out in the city assisting setting up the school as an excuse to get close to one of the teachers the Duchess had brought with her.

The Commodore's comments in his log prior to Gia bringing him down to the planet spoke of his intentions to follow orders and have his Marines remove Soraya Khan from the planet if she further refused to comply with orders.

Video of Gia on the bridge of the Bridgeport, then later in the Bridgeport's Conference room showed the Commodore was trapped by an alien lifeform that gave him no option but to go to the planets surface and see what the condition of the humans on the planet was like.

Cyril blinked out then returned a few minutes later with Doctor Mullins who testified that the conditions on the planet were reaching a point where disease would soon have taken over and very possibly wiped out a majority of its inhabitants if she had not interceded with the help of Gia convincing the people to cooperate.

When one of the Ministers asked why the Commodore violated the Alien Species Act by sending Soraya down to assist in the rebellion, which also violated several other Fleet and Federation laws, Gia produced the micro-disk on the rapes and suicides of the young girls and some males. This time she did not shut the holo-vid down as she had for the Commodore but ran it in its entirety.

For several minutes after the video ended it was silent in the room as one Minister had tears on his cheeks in seeing how the youth of this world was treated.

Then came the question she was expecting.

"How did this all come to be? The slaves, the treatment of female slaves, the treatment of both sexes by the King who should have been protecting them? How did this happen?" This was from Minister Seidel.

It was the Commodore who answered the question.

"Minister, from the log books and computer records we have been able to recover in a hidden room in the wall behind me with Gia's help, we have determined that part of the exploration workers were actually convicts, both male and female, who were sent to be labor on any newly discovered world. From what we could determine, at one point the convicts took over the settlement and put their overseers to work as slaves. It is thought that the perversion followed soon afterwards."

"There was a single comment in the log book of the Sequoia by it's Captain stating that the Monitor, the primary ship for the expedition had boosted from orbit, taking all the heavy equipment and technology with them except for the single computer we found in the hidden room. According to the search done by the Bridgeport concerning the Monitor, there is no record of it once it boosted from Ishtar. It is presumed lost in space."

Admiral Manafort asked if there were any other questions. Each Minister gave a negative answer before the Admiral spoke again.

"Yeoman Stratton make sure my words are properly logged. It is my decision that Commodore is guilty of violating several Fleet Regulations concerning the contact with the inhabitants of a new unassociated world. He is also guilty of utilizing Fleet assets without prior approval from Fleet Headquarters in the form of medical supplies and engineers and their equipment."

128

"But as I was reminded earlier, as we were taught in the Academy, often the commander on the scene must make decisions contrary to regulations, therefore, Commodore Faria's guilt in these matters is set aside due to circumstances beyond his control such as being unduly influenced by a previously unknown alien in the disguise of a Fleet Lieutenant Commander. The Commodore is therefore verbally admonished for not informing the Fleet of the aliens influence and his actions here on Phaedra."

"Minister Seidel, you are to take charge of your delegation vice Minister Cheever and file a report through my office which will then be sent to the Duke for further action if he deems it necessary. You will not have any contact with Parliament, especially President Swensen as it appears his actions are contrary to what your delegation was supposed to be dealing with. Do you have a complaint concerning my instructions Minister Seidel?"

"No Admiral, I have no complaint."

"Commodore Faria, I will remain in orbit for the next seven days. Submit a list of items you need to further improve the condition of our fellow humans here on Phaedra, and what we cannot supply directly off the ships in orbit, I shall direct the Fleet to supply as quickly as possible. This hearing is adjourned."

Seconds later everyone was back on the Avenger leaving the Commodore alone with Gia and Cyril. He turned to them.

"Well that went better than I could have hoped for. What now Gia since we now have the blessing of the Fleet to take care of these people?"

"Commodore, my mission is complete. Now it is up to my Father and the Council to determine what happens next, but Cyril and I have a lot of time to make up for, so hopefully we can stay here for a time."

"I take it the reason for your resignation is bogus?"

"Yes Sir, it is, but it is one that the Fleet readily accepts."

"Well I need to find Eli and Roman, so I can get the list the Admiral wants made out as quickly as possible."

Gia and Cyril vanished causing the Commodore to laugh as he left to find Eli.

In their quarters Cyril asked Gia what reason she gave for leaving the Fleet.

"I stated I was with child."

"Are you?"

"No, and there is no way they can know otherwise."

"Is there a child in the near future?"

"No as we have plenty of time for that later. Right now, I just want to be with you before we take that step."

A New Mission

Four days after Commodore Faria's disciplinary hearing, a meeting was held in the Council's Meeting Room with the Council of Phaedra, Admiral Manafort, Commodore Faria, Gia and Cyril, along with the Duchess before she boosted on her return to Keres.

The purpose of the meeting was for Karlie to lay out what she had planned for her charities and what, if any, help the Fleet or the locals could give to get the programs moving in the direction intended.

Karlie was laying out the plans for educating and helping unwed mothers when Gia nearly jumped from her chair. Everyone looked at Gia as she was standing still as if she was frozen.

"Gia, what's wrong?" Cyril asked.

"My Father. He's here."

Suddenly a man appeared behind Karlie's chair, a man who those not from Phaedra knew too well and Karlie had married.

"Alright, what the hell is going on?" The Duke spoke with a touch of anger in his voice.

"Gia, what are you doing?" Karlie asked.

"Duchess, I don't have that level of power to bring the Duke here, but my Father does."

"That's right daughter." A voice spoke from the other end of the room.

Everyone turned towards the voice to see a majestic looking older gentleman dressed in silver-grey robes with flowing white hair.

"Father, what are you doing bringing the Duke here without warning?"

131

"Making a point and hopefully closing the gap between our races. The Sakhalin are on the move and it is time for our human brothers and sisters to prepare for them."

Her Father made a motion with his hand and a creature appeared in the room that stood over two meters tall and to the humans familiar with Earth insects, it looked like a black Praying Mantis. He spoke again.

"Since my daughter has not introduced us, I am called Falkor, I set at the head of the Council of Delphi. Duke Thomas, my apologizes for meeting you this way, but if not for the Sakhalin, we might not meet for years."

"Lord Falkor, I accept your reasoning."

Gia walked over to her Father and hugged him then kissed him on his cheek.

"Father, it is good to see you even under these circumstances. But please state your intentions as those who work in the Palace on Keres will soon panic if the Duke does not return soon."

"Daughter, they will not even know he was gone."

"Lord Falkor, I was having a meeting with the Federation Council on Keres when you brought me here. There are a dozen people that saw me vanish from the Conference room." The Duke brought up."

"Duke Thomas, time no longer exists within that room, so no one has yet recognized you are missing. Now let's get down to business."

"Please do."

"Daughter, there is one last task I would like you to undertake with Cyril at your side."

"What is that Father?"

"Daughter, the Council agrees with me that with the expansion of the Federation, it is time that the Delphi are represented before the Throne and with your knowledge and experience as a Fleet officer, I would appreciate your acceptance as our Ambassador to the Hanover Throne."

Before she could answer, Karlie spoke up.

"Gia, I'm sure I speak for my husband when I say your attendance at Court would be a pleasure and your Father is correct in that we need to have someone who understands us simple humans as we venture further into space."

"Yes, my bride said it better than I could." The Duke commented.

"Duke Thomas, I take your words as acceptance of Princess Gia of Delphi as our Ambassador?"

"Yes Falkor, I do accept the Princess as the Ambassador from Delphi."

"Good, we shall meet again."

With that the Duke disappeared.

"Daughter, I am aware that your powers are not up to transporting yourself to Keres, so a Delphian ship will shortly arrive to act as your personal vessel to take yourself and Cyril to Keres. It will return to Delphi once you are comfortable on Keres but available if needed."

"I understand Father, and I accept this task my King."

"Thank you. Now I shall depart and allow this meeting to continue. Good day to all."

Falkor bent over and kissed Gia on both cheeks then vanished. Gia stood for a second looking in the direction her Father had stood before turning back to the table. Cyril was grinning at what had just happened.

"Shut up Cyril, we'll talk about this later." She told him.

He laughed out loud at her comment.

"Gia, did you just call your Father, King?"

"Yes Duchess, my father is also our King."

"This will make for interesting conversation around the Court. So where were we when the King interrupted us?" Karlie commented.

Later that evening, the Duchess hosted a dinner on the Intrepid for the Admiral, the Commodore, Gia and Cyril before she boosted for Keres. During the dessert coffee, Karlie asked Gia a question she had held since they first met.

"Gia, I've heard you reference Cyril being in exile for a thousand years. How long is that in comparison to an Earth Solar Year?"

Gia sipped on her wine as Cyril lightly chuckled before Gia answered.

"Karlie, Delphi is a mirror of Earth in rotation and orbit."

"Are you saying a thousand years is just that?"

"Yes Karlie, it is just that."

"How old are you?"

"Yes, my love, how old are you?" Cyril joked.

Cyril yelped when Gia stuck him in the side with a raptor claw.

"Duchess, I am three thousand, seven hundred, and twenty-three years old by your calendar."

"Forgive me Gia, but you don't look like you are much more then twenty-five in your natural form." Admiral Manafort commented.

"Admiral, in comparison to human norm, I'm only fifteen even if I do look older. We age at a different rate of course than humans and we mature at a different rate since we have such longevity."

"Are you immortal?" The Commodore asked.

"No Commodore, we are not immortal. In human form I could have been killed as any human if my skills were not superior to those who opposed me. In this form, it takes much more but it is possible."

"I'll not ask how much more as that should be a secret we humans should never know."

"Thank you, Commodore, as that keeps me from telling you it is none of your business." She said with a smile.

Everyone laughed, and the conversation turned to Gia going to Keres.

Keres

As the time drew close for Gia to leave Phaedra, meetings were being held almost daily as the Fleets Intelligence personnel form the ships above searched every line of the hard copy documents in the hidden room, and every byte of information from the computer once they were able to get it powered up and the old operating system to cooperate. Now where could it be found the reason for burying the ship under the castle, or the weapons removed from it, then sealing the door.

There would be many mysteries left for others to hopefully find the answers to once Gia and Cyril departed Phaedra. Cyril asked Gia one night if a Seer could be brought to learn why things had happened as they did. She told him that price was too high for such answers and she doubted her Father would allow it. Privately she was also afraid Cyril would learn things about his own history that had not surfaced in his memories as he was still coping with those he did carry.

Gia timed her arrival to coincide with Karlie's return to the Palace, arriving a day later. Delphian ships did not transit space as they just moved from point to point much like their masters did between locations on a planet.

The Duke ruled the Delphian Embassy would be different in function than the normal Federation planets embassy since there was no trade involved or exchange of Ambassadors involved.

When given a choice of location for the Delphian Embassy, Cyril asked if they could set it upon the high peak of the mountains where the Palace was located. The Duke approved the location and asked if they needed the assistance of Keres craftsmen to build the Embassy. Cyril just smiled and said it was already built. That night, tapping into Cyril's powers, Gia set wards on their home to prevent their own magic from leaking out and disrupting human activity as they would study and increase their own abilities.

A week later a formal dinner was held at the Palace to introduce Gia and Cyril to the Ambassadors to the Throne located on Keres. The new President of the Federation was also present as was the Federation Council. The Former President resigned when it was discovered that he hoped to cash in on the discovery of Phaedra by claiming an ancestor discovered the planet.

Gia dressed simply for this dinner until she saw how the other females attending were dressed. She stepped behind a curtain then returned dressed in a silvery gown which showed more skin than it concealed with a jeweled necklace accenting her breasts. Her hair was done in a fashion to insure her long ears were exposed with a wreath of small colored gems on her head.

Cyril was dressed in a military type uniform of silver with gold trim and knee high black boots.

She was announced as Princess Gia Khan and spent the evening talking to Ambassadors and their wives about Delphi which Gia had to hedge on her replies to prevent too much information getting out to the public.

One Ambassador, who looked more like a scholar than a politician, asked Gia if she had ever heard of the ancient Earth Myth of the Oracle of Delphi from ancient Greece. Gia said she had and they talked for nearly an hour as she explained her Father's Mother had told her that story when she was a young child. What she did not tell the gentleman was that her Grandmother was Phemonoe, the first of the Oracles as they were trying to guide the Greeks to betterment.

At every party she attended, if the gentleman was present, they would talk about Earth's ancient history. She learned through the Duchess, that this gentleman once taught Earth Myth and Lore at the University on Earth before becoming their Ambassador to the Throne.

Five months into time on Keres, Gia and Cyril went to the East Rim and arranged an understanding between the Mordi and the Federation. Buoys were set along the edge of the rim warning both sides not to cross into the others space, thus ending the long war. The Federation patrolled the rim to prevent prospectors from violating the agreement.

Gia became a common sight at dinner parties and at court as she never failed to respond to a request by the Duke when questions arose concerning the exploration of deep space. But she withheld much information that the Duke only learned of in his private office, secured from prying ears. In this she produced a holo-map of unknown space with areas blocked out to depict areas of danger from other alien species which he could call up as needed in his office.

A year after Gia assumed her role as Ambassador, another large dinner was held with her parents in attendance. King Falkor presented the Duke with a crystal ball in which he could contact Delphi much as the Hayutan crystals that were used to communicate with each other. When the Duke commented how much it was like the Hayutan crystals, the King smiled and told him who did he think taught the Hayutans how to construct theirs. It was then that he knew the Delphians had also infiltrated the ranks of humans much like the Hayutans had eons later on. The Duke did not ask the King if there were Delphians hidden amongst the human race still yet.

The Delphi also gave the Federation the ability to neutralize the Tranter's cloaking ability which they used to capture human vessels and capture the crews for their breeding farms. The Fleet caught three Tranter ships entering into Federation space and destroyed them utilizing the fighters their destroyers and cruisers carried. The Tranters had became use to entering and leaving Federation space at will due to their cloaking technology, but with the ability of the Fleet to neutralize that advantage, plus the small and agile fighters, the Tranters learned to stay out of Federation space.

The Sakhalin were a different problem in that they did not capture humans for food, but killed them for fertilizer for their own fields back in their home systems. The planets the humans occupied were stripped of all vegetation for food stores before moving to

138

another Class M planet. It would take six months of running battles between space vessels before the Fleet finally stopped the Sakhalin advance, and as with the Mordi, came to an agreement of boundary lines with them. Again, it was Gia and Cyril who were able to act as negotiators in establishing that shaky peace between the Sakhalin and the Federation.

Gia served three Dukes, over one hundred years before she decided to give Cyril children. She gave birth to twin girls which she named Karlie after the Duchess who had since passed on and Ganieda, the name of one of Gia's early friends on Delphi. They would be the first of a dozen children to keep them busy, teaching and guiding them in the ways of the Delphi as their own powers increase with study and practice.

Life for Gia and Cyril was not without adventures, but those tales are for a different telling.

Page Left Blank

About the Author

Leon Michaels is the author of several novels and short stories that reflect his twenty-three years of military service.   Michaels enlisted in the Marine Corps in 1970 and has memberships in the Veterans of Foreign Wars, the American Legion, the Disabled American Veterans organizations, NRA, and Rotary International.   In 1971, he married his high school sweetheart, raised three daughters and has three grandsons. He calls Creek County, Oklahoma home.

Made in the USA
Middletown, DE
23 September 2018